FROM SHADOW TO SUNSHINE

ADITI JAIN

Aditi Jain, a 19-year-old author, has made a remarkable entry in the literary world with her debut novel, "From Shadow to Sunshine". Inspired by her own experiences and observations, she penned a captivating tale of trauma, resilience, and personal growth. With sensitivity, Aditi explores life's ups and downs, complexities of relationships, and the power of human spirit. Through her writing, she aims to inspire and support others who have faced similar challenges, encouraging open conversations about mental health and wellness. This book offers a relatable and thought-provoking journey to readers of all ages.

Contents

Preface

Emma's emotional journey is a reminder that life's challenges are unavoidable, but transformation and growth are always within reach. Her story was like a stormy night, filled with darkness and uncertainty. During her lowest point, Emma felt overwhelmed and lost, much like a stormy night with dark clouds and strong winds.

Yet, even in the midst of that tempest, there was a glimmer of hope, a promise that the storm would pass, and the sun would rise again.The turning point in Emma's journey marked the dawn of a new era, a fresh beginning, and a chance to start anew. The sunrise symbolized the triumph of hope over despair, of light over darkness. It signifies a moment of clarity and a shift in her emotional state towards positivity and growth.

Emma's story serves as a powerful reminder that everyone's emotional journey is unique. We've all faced storms in our lives but in those moments of darkness, we discover our inner strength, our capacity for growth, and our resilience.

Just as every storm eventually gives way to sunshine, our struggles can yield to hope, renewal, and transformation. Emma's journey shows us that no matter how bleak the circumstances may seem, there's always a sunrise on the horizon, waiting to illuminate our path and guide us towards a brighter future.

Acknowledgements

As I pen down these words, I am filled with gratitude and love for the two people who have been my rock, my guiding light, and my biggest cheerleaders. To my esteemed parents, Mr. Dharmendra Jain & Mrs. Kalpna Jain, I am honored to dedicate this work to you both, with all my love. Thank you, for being my everything.

Now, I would like to express my deepest gratitude to Manorath Rastogi for your invaluable assistance and steadfast support throughout the writing process. Your guidance and feedback have been instrumental in shaping this novel.

A special thanks to Mahatav bhaiya for the stunning cover page design that beautifully captures the essence of the story. Your creative vision has truly enhanced the overall presentation of the novel.

And I extend my heartfelt appreciation to Rohit Shukla and Aarushi Sharma for their constant support and encouragement. Your belief in me has been a source of strength and inspiration.

To all of you, I am immensely grateful for your contributions and presence in this creative journey. Your support has made a significant impact on the completion of this novel.

With love and gratitude,
Aditi Jain

Emma Parker, a ten-year-old girl in the 5th grade, lived in Lambeth, UK.

Most may not know much about Lambeth, so here's a glimpse into this vibrant borough:

Lambeth, situated along the banks of the River Thames, boasts a rich cultural heritage and a diverse community. Renowned landmarks like The London Eye, South Bank Centre, and Lambeth Palace are found here. Lambeth Palace, dating back to the 13th century, is the official residence of the Archbishop of Canterbury, noted for its architectural beauty and historical significance. The South Bank Centre, a bustling cultural complex, hosts numerous arts and entertainment events. The London Eye, one of the world's largest observation wheels, offers a panoramic view of London. Lambeth's streets are lively, filled with local markets, street performers, and cultural festivals. Parks like Brockwell and Kennington provide green spaces for relaxation and recreation. The community is friendly and welcoming, coming together to celebrate every event and festival. Lambeth's diverse culture and rich history make it a unique and interesting place.

Emma's Family and Personality

Emma lived with her small, loving family, bound by strong ties of love and support. They were always there for each other, offering encouragement and understanding in times of need. This special bond brought them closer together. Her father, John, was a dedicated architect who often brought home sketches of buildings he was designing. Her mother, Sarah, was a compassionate nurse who worked at a nearby hospital, always sharing stories of the lives she touched. Together, they created a nurturing environment for Emma and her younger sister, Ammy.

Emma was a unique blend of intelligence, determination, and ambition. Her consistent top grades set her apart from her peers, and she was known not just for her academic performance but also for her ambitious dreams. A kind girl, Emma was always down to earth and treated everyone with respect. Her energy and curiosity, paired with her bright smile, brought joy and playfulness to the family. Emma loved reading books, exploring new ideas, and helping others. She was often seen with her nose in a book, lost in the worlds created by her favorite authors. Despite her young age, she had a clear vision of what she wanted to achieve in life.

A Morning in the Parker Household

One bright morning, the sun peeked through the curtains of Emma's room, casting a warm glow on her collection of books and posters of her favorite characters. She woke up with a sense of excitement, ready to embrace the day. After getting dressed in her neatly pressed school uniform, Emma headed downstairs for breakfast, the aroma of freshly made pancakes filling the air.

"Good morning, Emma!" Sarah greeted her with a warm smile as she flipped another pancake onto a plate. "I made your favorite today."

"Thanks, Mom!" Emma replied, taking a seat at the table and pouring herself a glass of orange juice. "It smells delicious!"

Just as she was about to take her first bite, a faint sound caught her attention. It was the sound of crying coming from the room next door. Emma's heart sank. She recognized that cry—it was her younger sister, Ammy. Quickly setting down her fork, Emma excused herself and rushed to Ammy's room.

Comforting Ammy

Ammy, just three years old, was sitting on her bed, tears streaming down her cheeks. Her favorite teddy bear lay on the floor, seemingly abandoned. Emma knelt down beside her sister and gently picked her up, cradling her in her arms.

"Shh, it's okay, Ammy. I'm here," Emma whispered, stroking her sister's hair. "Why are you crying?"

Emma said firmly, "Mom, it seems Ammy is hungry. Get breakfast ready quickly." After saying this, she went downstairs with Ammy and made her sit on the chair at the dinner table. Her mother, Sarah, made Ammy's favorite breakfast and served it to her with a glass of milk. She fed Ammy with love, and they both enjoyed their meal together happily.

As they ate, Emma suddenly asked her mother about Ammy's admission. It was an unexpected question, but crucial nonetheless. Sarah had been contemplating enrolling Ammy in kindergarten, a significant decision considering Ammy's age, readiness for school, and the kindergarten's curriculum.

Her mother replied thoughtfully, "Yes, I think we should. It's time she starts her educational journey."

A few days later, Sarah enrolled Ammy in Emma's school. Both sisters now went to school together, sharing the morning walks and schoolyard adventures. The memories they created during their school days were filled with laughter and shared experiences. Despite occasional sibling squabbles, they shared a special bond of love and friendship.

As the school year progressed, final exams approached. Both sisters were preparing diligently, supporting each other through the stress. But suddenly, one day, Emma started feeling unwell. She avoided food and slept more than usual, which concerned Sarah deeply. She advised Emma to stay hydrated and offered her light, easy-to-eat food, but her condition persisted.

Seeing no improvement, Sarah and John decided to seek medical attention for Emma. They booked an appointment with a specialist. Leaving Ammy at home with their maid, they took Emma to the hospital. On the way, Emma was filled with anxiety, finding it hard to deal with health concerns and academic pressure simultaneously. But Sarah offered words of encouragement, providing a strong support system.

At the hospital, Emma's anxiety grew. She received a call from the maid but chose to ignore it, focusing on the consultation. The doctor ordered several medical tests, including a Complete Blood Count (CBC) and a Widal test, to diagnose her condition accurately. Emma underwent the tests, and the results revealed she had typhoid, caused by the Salmonella typhi virus. The diagnosis added another layer of anxiety, but her parents reassured her, providing comfort and encouragement in this challenging time.

Back home, they were greeted by Ammy's loud cries. Overwhelmed by the day's events, Sarah's emotions ran high, and she scolded the maid. John quickly intervened, calming Sarah and suggesting they address the situation calmly.

Sarah picked up Ammy, soothing her, and took her to Emma's bedroom to help Emma fall asleep. The comforting hug and familiar surroundings helped Emma drift into a peaceful slumber. Though Emma slept, Sarah remained awake, worried and overwhelmed by everything that had happened. It was a stressful time, especially with both daughters' exams the next day.

Emma woke up early, her sleep restless and filled with anxiety about the upcoming exam. She found her mother already awake and hugged her tightly. Despite not having slept all night, Sarah didn't let Emma know, instead kissing her forehead—a gesture of deep love and reassurance. Emma cherished the moment, feeling her mother's unwavering support.

After a quick wash, Emma joined her mother in the kitchen, where Sarah was preparing breakfast. Soon, Ammy woke up, and Sarah got her ready for school. John, too, was getting ready to drop his daughters off. The house buzzed with the morning hustle as everyone prepared for the day ahead.

After breakfast, John drove Emma and Ammy to school. He stopped the car in front of the school and stepped out, wishing them "good luck" with a warm smile. His words of encouragement uplifted both girls, giving them the confidence to face their exams.

Emma, though nervous, walked to her class, recalling her mother's words: "Emma, believe in yourself and do your best.

Remember, hard work pays off, and I'm proud of you no matter what." These words boosted her confidence. She began her exam, managing her time carefully, glancing at her watch to ensure she allocated enough time for each question.

Despite her health concerns, Emma was determined to give her best effort, her family's love and support echoing in her mind as she worked through each question.

During her exam, Emma glanced at her watch, only to realize it had stopped. Panic threatened to overwhelm her as she thought, "Oh no, how will I manage my time now?" Despite the initial anxiety, she took a deep breath, calming herself. She decided to face any challenges with resilience and determination, pushing aside ominous thoughts.

After the exam, as they left the school, Emma saw her father waiting patiently. Ammy rushed joyfully to him, but Emma approached with disappointment written on her face. Concerned, her father asked, "What happened, my love? Why are you upset?"

Emma sighed, "I didn't do well on my exam. I'm disappointed in myself."

Her father gently replied, "Emma, I understand things didn't go as planned, but it's okay."

Emma explained, "I was so exhausted and couldn't concentrate properly. I wish I could have done better, but my health wasn't cooperating. I'm trying not to be too hard on myself, but it's frustrating knowing I could have done more."

Her father reassured her, "Your health is the priority right now, and I'm proud of how hard you've worked despite feeling unwell. Take this time to rest and take care of yourself. You're strong and capable, and I believe in you, my sweetheart."

Back home, the familiar surroundings brought Emma comfort. She changed out of her uniform and joined her family for lunch. Her mother, Sarah, lovingly served lunch and engaged both Emma and Ammy in conversation. Sarah's supportive presence uplifted Emma's spirits, reminding her to stay positive and face challenges with courage.

Emma felt fortunate to have such a supportive family who stood by her through every hurdle. Her parents were her biggest cheerleaders, constantly encouraging her and reminding her that one exam didn't define her abilities or success. Emma also leaned on a circle of supportive friends who provided positive energy and encouragement.

As they enjoyed dinner together, Emma's mood lightened, and her parents felt relieved to see her happy after a challenging time with her health and exams. Emma retreated to her room after dinner, dedicated to preparing for her next exam. Her commitment showed progress in her studies, and with each exam, Emma's confidence grew.

Finally, after weeks of exams, Emma completed her last paper. She reflected on her journey, grateful for her family's unwavering support and her own determination. Despite the challenges, Emma emerged stronger and more resilient, ready to face whatever the future held.

2

Emma was finally able to relax after the stress of her exams, spending quality time with her family. She cherished these moments, knowing how important it was to unwind and destress after the intense period of studying and exams. Emma savored every moment of her well-deserved relaxation, enjoying the simple pleasures of being with her loved ones without the pressure of schoolwork hanging over her.

As evening approached, they decided to have dinner outside, opting for a change of scenery and a meal in the open air. Emma suggested going to her favorite restaurant, a stunning venue known for its grand architecture and cozy ambiance. Excitement filled the air as they set out for the evening, looking forward to a delicious meal and a long drive afterward to explore new places and enjoy each other's company.

Arriving at the restaurant, Ammy's wide-eyed wonder at the grandeur of the place was priceless. The majestic architecture and inviting ambiance captivated her, making the dining experience all the more special. They settled in, ordered their favorite dishes, and enjoyed a wonderful surprise of exquisite cuisine in such a remarkable setting.

After their satisfying meal, they embarked on a long drive, filled with anticipation about where the road might take them. The sense of adventure and the joy of being together as a family added to their excitement.

Heading home after a fun-filled outing, Ammy soon fell asleep on her mother's lap in the car. Meanwhile, Emma excitedly recounted the highlights of the evening with her parents. However, her joy was momentarily tempered when she noticed a broken traffic signal along the way, prompting her to ask about a recent accident in the area.

Sarah, Emma's mother, began to recount the incident, her voice tinged with concern. "One sunny morning," she began, "as the vendors were setting up their stalls and the aroma of freshly baked goods filled the air, a sudden commotion shattered the usual tranquility. A young girl named Romy, who worked at a nearby fruit shop, witnessed a stray dog darting across the street, followed closely by a speeding car."

"In a split second," Sarah continued, "the car swerved to avoid the dog but lost control, crashing into Romy's fruit stand. Crates of apples went flying, causing chaos in the bustling marketplace."

Emma listened intently, her heart going out to the girl named Romy and her family. She understood the fragility of life and the unexpected challenges that could arise in everyday situations. As they neared home, she reflected on the day's adventures, grateful for their safety and the precious time spent together as a family.

Emma asked in shock, "Mom, what happened next?"

Her mother's eyes softened with empathy as she continued, "Then, people around them quickly gathered to support those affected by the accident. The next day, the community came together to clean up the mess, tend to the injured, and ensure everyone's safety."

Emma's heart raced with fear upon hearing about the accident, and she felt a knot tighten in her chest. She turned to her mother, her voice trembling, "Mom, I feel scared." Her mother immediately sensed Emma's anxiety and lovingly placed her hand on Emma's head, offering her comfort. "What's wrong, my sweetheart? Why are you so scared?" She handed Emma a glass of water, gently urging her to take a sip. "Emma, I know hearing about real accidents can be frightening, but remember, accidents happen. It's important to stay strong and not let fear take over. Instead, you can learn from these experiences and grow stronger. Take a deep breath, stay calm, my dear."

Emma nodded, trying to steady her breathing and calm her racing thoughts. She found solace in her mother's reassuring words and the warmth of her presence. As they continued their journey home, the evening grew serene, the sun dipping below the horizon as they exchanged tales and laughter. Every step felt like a shared adventure, drawing them closer to the comfort of their own sanctuary.

Upon reaching home, Emma's mother gently encouraged her to rest. "It's already late, Emma. You should get some sleep," she said softly. Emma, however, found it difficult to shake off the lingering thoughts of the broken traffic signal and the accident. Her mind spun in circles, replaying the moments over and over again, the fear weighing heavily on her.

Despite her racing thoughts, exhaustion eventually took over, and Emma drifted into a restless sleep. Her dreams were filled with fleeting images of chaos and reassurance, a blend of fear and the comforting presence of her family. The night passed slowly, the soft glow of the moon casting a calming light over their home, offering a quiet reassurance amidst Emma's turbulent thoughts.

The next morning, Emma woke up feeling a bit unsettled after a night of deep thinking. Her mind was still grappling with the lingering thoughts from the previous evening, but she tried to push them aside as she went about her morning routine. She joined her family for breakfast, trying to appear cheerful despite feeling somewhat preoccupied.

During breakfast, her father noticed that Emma seemed distant and asked with concern, "Are you okay, Emma?" She forced a smile and replied, "Yes, Dad, I'm fine. Don't worry."

As they finished their meal, Emma's parents made an exciting announcement about their upcoming trip from Lambeth, UK to Barcelona, Spain. Barcelona, known for its vibrant culture, stunning architecture like the Sagrada Familia, delicious cuisine including paella and tapas, and beautiful beaches, was a captivating destination awaiting them. Ammy, brimming with enthusiasm, eagerly embraced the idea of the trip, but Emma struggled to match her sister's excitement. Despite her reservations, Emma kept her feelings to herself, understanding that it was her parents' decision and feeling obliged to go along with their plans.

Retreating to her room after breakfast, Emma began packing for the trip. Her mind was divided between the practicalities of packing and her lingering uncertainty about the journey ahead. Despite her initial reluctance, everything moved swiftly with the trip preparations. Tickets were booked, last-minute arrangements were made, and the next day arrived with an early morning start for their flight at 8 AM.

At the airport, the family navigated through check-in and security screening, finally settling into the boarding area. Emma observed Ammy's excitement about her first flight, contrasting it with her own mixed feelings. She found herself feeling nervous and unsure, not yet embracing the anticipation and thrill of the upcoming adventure. Emma knew she needed time to adjust and find her own excitement amidst her apprehensions.

As they boarded the plane and settled into their seats, Emma continued to put on a brave face for her parents' sake, masking her inner reservations. She hoped that as the journey progressed, she would gradually warm up to the idea and begin to appreciate the experience as much as her family did. Deep down, Emma knew that despite her initial reluctance, this trip could bring unexpected joys and discoveries, and she was determined to keep an open mind as they embarked on their journey to Barcelona.

It sounds like Emma and her family had quite an eventful journey, from the excitement of flying to Barcelona to the unexpected turn of events upon their return. Let's continue from where the car accident occurred:

The sudden jolt as the car overturned left Emma disoriented and in shock. The world around her spun for a moment before everything went dark. Her mother, who had fallen on the road in the chaos, struggled to regain her composure and rushed to Emma's side. Emma's father, dazed but unhurt, quickly assessed the situation and called for emergency assistance. Minutes felt like hours until finally the sound of the ambulance siren filled the air.

Paramedics arrived at the scene. They carefully extracted Emma and her mother from the car wreckage, ensuring they received immediate medical attention.

The paramedics provided initial medical aid on the spot before transporting Emma and her mother to the nearest hospital for further evaluation. Emma's father, still in shock from the accident, accompanied them, his thoughts a whirlwind of concern and relief that they had survived such a frightening ordeal.

At the hospital, Emma underwent a series of examinations to assess her injuries. She had sustained minor cuts and bruises, but the real concern was her emotional state. The trauma of the accident, coupled with her previous anxieties, had taken a toll on her. The medical team ensured she received both physical and psychological care to help her recover from the shock.

Meanwhile, Emma's mother, though shaken and bruised, remained strong for her daughter. She reassured Emma, holding back her own fears, and stayed by her side throughout the examinations and treatments. Emma's father, grappling with a mix of guilt and relief, supported both Emma and her mother as they navigated through this unexpected crisis.

Hours passed as Emma underwent observations and treatments. Gradually, she began to feel more stable, both physically and emotionally. The hospital staff provided a comforting environment, and Emma found solace in the presence of her family despite the circumstances.

The aftermath of the accident was indeed overwhelming and fraught with uncertainty for Emma and her family. Here's how the situation unfolded:

The moments after the car overturned were filled with chaos and urgency. Emma's father, shaken but composed, immediately called for an ambulance. Every passing second felt like an eternity as they waited for help to arrive. The sound of the approaching ambulance siren was a welcome relief amidst the turmoil.

Emergency responders acted swiftly upon arrival, assessing the situation and providing initial medical aid on the scene. They carefully extracted Emma and her mother from the wreckage, prioritizing their safety and stabilization. The paramedics' professionalism and quick actions were crucial in ensuring that Emma and her mother received prompt medical attention.

At the hospital, medical professionals worked tirelessly to address Emma and her mother's injuries. The doctors and nurses provided thorough examinations, administered treatments, and closely monitored their conditions. The medical team's expertise and dedication played a pivotal role in stabilizing Emma and her mother amidst the trauma of the accident.

For Emma and her family, the emotional toll was profound. The suddenness and severity of the accident left them physically injured and emotionally drained. Fear and anxiety gripped them as they grappled with the aftermath of such a traumatic event. Coping with the uncertainties and challenges brought about by the accident was a daunting task, requiring strength and resilience.

Despite the fear and uncertainty, Emma found solace in the presence of her family. Her mother's unwavering support and her father's calm reassurance provided a sense of stability amidst the turmoil. Together, they navigated through the difficult hours in the hospital, drawing strength from each other's presence and support.

As the night wore on, Emma and her mother's conditions stabilized, and the medical team determined it was safe for them to be discharged with instructions for continued care at home. Emma's father ensured they had everything they needed for their recovery, grateful for the swift response of the emergency services and the compassionate care provided by the hospital staff.

Returning home brought a mix of relief and reflection for Emma and her family. The accident had left an indelible mark, reminding them of the fragility of life and the importance of cherishing each moment together. In the days that followed, they focused on healing both physically and emotionally, finding strength in their bond and the support of their community.

3

Emma's journey to recovery was fraught with unsettling moments. As she woke from her unconscious state, her mind struggled to piece together the fragments of her memory. The disorientation and grogginess weighed heavily on her, making it difficult to grasp the present moment. Her parents, ever vigilant and supportive, sought medical assistance to ensure Emma received the care she needed.

The doctor's reassuring words provided a glimmer of hope amidst the uncertainty. Despite Emma's initial confusion, her gradual awakening was a positive sign of her body's resilience. Her parents, relieved by the doctor's assessment, continued to provide unwavering support, knowing that time and patience were crucial in Emma's recovery process.

Nighttime brought its own challenges as Emma grappled with haunting nightmares. The vivid imagery of past memories—like the stopped watch and broken traffic signal—seemed to intertwine with her recent ordeal. Each memory felt like a piece of a puzzle, hinting at connections she couldn't yet fully understand. Despite her fear and unease, Emma's determination to unravel these mysteries fueled her introspection.

In the quiet moments of the night, Emma found herself drawn into deep contemplation. She lay awake, thoughts swirling, as she searched for meaning in the chaos of her memories. Her hands trembled as she reached for a glass of water, the physical manifestation of her inner turmoil.

As Emma lay back down, the weight of her thoughts pressed upon her. The silence of the night enveloped her, offering both solace and an eerie backdrop to her reflections. It was a pivotal moment in Emma's journey—a time of introspection and introspective.

Emma's heart ached with the absence of Ammy, her thoughts continuously circling around her sister's whereabouts. The morning brought with it a restless urgency to seek answers, and when Emma finally confronted her mother, the explanation provided only deepened her confusion. Her mother's reassurances were met with a growing skepticism as doubts gnawed at Emma's mind.

Despite the unsettling thoughts about Ammy, Emma found solace in her mother's efforts to comfort her. The familiar aroma of her favorite breakfast momentarily lifted her spirits, a small gesture that reminded Emma of the love and care that permeated their home.

As the days passed and Emma prepared for the new school session, her desire to reunite with Ammy intensified. The bond between the sisters had always been strong, and Emma's determination to be with Ammy grew stronger with each passing day.

In a moment of reflection, Emma drifted off to sleep, only to awaken to the late afternoon sun filtering through her window. The clock read 5 PM, and Emma's instinct led her to the kitchen, expecting to find her mother. Yet, her search within the house yielded no sign of her.

Stepping outside, Emma called out, her voice carrying across the tranquil garden. There, amidst the blooms and serenity, Emma spotted her mother. Without hesitation, she joined her, the shared moment in the garden becoming a quiet refuge amidst the tumult of Emma's thoughts.

Emma woke up the next morning feeling drained from the previous day's emotional rollercoaster. The weight of loneliness and isolation seemed heavier as she prepared herself for another day at school. Despite her efforts to hide her inner turmoil, the facade of a smile she wore for her parents masked the pain she carried inside.

At school, Emma found herself navigating through the hallways with a sense of detachment. The familiar faces of her peers seemed distant, their conversations fading into background noise as she tried to focus on her studies. The lingering fear from her accident lingered, heightening her anxiety with every step she took.

During lunchtime, Emma sat alone in a quiet corner of the cafeteria. The once bustling room now felt like an echo chamber of isolation. Her mind raced with thoughts of her friends drifting away and the daunting prospect of rebuilding connections. Despite her efforts to engage, Emma struggled to find the courage to approach her peers, fearing rejection and misunderstanding.

As the school day drew to a close, Emma's longing for familiarity intensified. She yearned for the warmth of friendships that once felt secure and comforting. Walking home, she replayed the events of the day, grappling with the ache of loneliness that pierced her heart.

Arriving home, Emma greeted her parents with a faint smile, masking the turmoil brewing beneath the surface. She shared a quiet dinner with them, their presence offering a fleeting sense of solace amidst the storm raging within her. Emma's ability to shield her parents from her struggles showcased her strength and determination to protect their happiness.

Retreating to her room, Emma sought refuge in the silence. She dimmed the lights and lay on her bed, enveloped in thoughts that weighed heavily on her mind. Tears welled up as she confronted the harsh reality of feeling alone in a crowd. The night stretched on, each moment marked by the ache of longing and the silent tears that spoke volumes of her silent battle.

In the solitude of her room, Emma found herself grappling with the complexities of friendship, identity, and resilience. As she drifted into sleep, she hoped for a glimmer of light amidst the darkness, a beacon of hope that would guide her through the challenges ahead.

Emma's days at school became a stark reminder of her growing solitude. Each morning, she masked her inner turmoil behind a facade of composure, unwilling to burden her parents with her struggles. The routine of preparing for school and exchanging brief pleasantries with her family felt increasingly hollow, the weight of her loneliness pressing down upon her.

Arriving at school, Emma navigated the corridors with a sense of detachment, the echoes of laughter and camaraderie among her peers amplifying her sense of isolation. The familiar routine of classes offered a brief respite, yet the moments between classes stretched on like endless voids of emptiness.

During lunchtime, Emma found herself retreating to a solitary corner of the cafeteria, aching to connect with someone yet unable to bridge the gap between herself and her classmates. The sight of her peers chatting animatedly in their cliques only served to deepen her sense of alienation. The food on her tray remained untouched as tears welled up, the weight of loneliness settling heavily upon her shoulders.

Yearning for a reprieve, Emma sought solace in the outdoor games she once cherished. As she arrived at the football field, a stark realization dawned upon her — there was no one to play with, no friendly faces to share in the joy of the game. The bitter sting of abandonment pierced her heart, leaving her feeling betrayed and utterly alone.

The indifference and exclusion from her classmates cut deeper than she ever imagined. Emma struggled to reconcile the reality of her isolation with the memories of friendship and camaraderie she once cherished. The overwhelming sense of abandonment left her questioning her self-worth and her place among her peers.

In the midst of her turmoil, Emma grappled with the harsh truth that she was alone in facing these challenges. The longing for connection, for understanding, remained unfulfilled as she navigated each day with a heavy heart and a fragile spirit.

Emma's outburst echoed through the room, her voice trembling with raw emotion. The weight of her words hung heavily in the air, a stark contrast to her mother's attempts to reassure her. Her mother's expression softened, a mixture of concern and disbelief at Emma's accusation.

"Emma, sweetheart, where did you hear this?" Her mother's voice wavered, trying to maintain composure amidst Emma's anguish.

"I heard it at school," Emma replied, her voice choked with tears. "Those girls were gossiping about Ammy, saying she's gone. How could they say such things?"

Her mother's eyes filled with sadness as she reached out to hold Emma's trembling hands. "Oh, Emma," she sighed heavily, struggling to find the right words. "Those girls must have misunderstood something. Ammy is safe, she's with your aunt. I promise you."

Emma withdrew her hands, her eyes pleading for honesty. "Mom, please stop lying to me," she pleaded, her voice breaking. "I know something happened to Ammy. Why won't you tell me the truth?"

Her mother's shoulders slumped, torn between protecting Emma and acknowledging her fears. "Emma, I'm not lying to you," she insisted softly. "I don't know where this rumor came from, but I assure you, Ammy is fine."

Emma's resolve hardened as she struggled to reconcile her mother's words with the unsettling gossip she had heard. "I need to know the truth," she insisted, her voice wavering but firm. "Please, Mom."

Her mother sighed deeply, her gaze filled with compassion and sorrow. "Emma, I understand you're scared and confused," she began gently, "but sometimes rumors can be hurtful and untrue. Ammy is safe, I promise you."

Emma's heart ached with uncertainty and fear. Despite her mother's reassurances, doubts gnawed at her, fueled by the unsettling gossip she couldn't shake off. She longed for clarity, for a tangible reassurance that her sister was indeed safe.

The tension in the room lingered as Emma and her mother sat in uneasy silence, grappling with the weight of unspoken truths and unanswered questions. The bond between them strained under the weight of Emma's anguish and her mother's attempts to shield her from harsh realities.

Emma's decision to change schools weighed heavily on her mind as she prepared to broach the subject with her parents. Despite her inner turmoil, she knew it was a necessary step towards finding a healthier environment for herself. That evening, after dinner, Emma gathered her courage and approached her parents in the living room.

"Mom, Dad," Emma began tentatively, her voice trembling slightly. "I've been thinking a lot lately, and I feel like... I need to change schools."

Her parents exchanged concerned glances, their expressions reflecting a mix of worry and empathy for Emma's struggle. Her father spoke first, his tone gentle yet filled with concern. "Emma, sweetheart, is everything okay at your current school?"

Emma took a deep breath, trying to steady her nerves. "I've been feeling really unhappy there," she admitted, her voice wavering. "It's been hard for me to cope, especially after everything that's happened."

Her mother's eyes softened with understanding as she reached out to hold Emma's hand. "We want what's best for you, Emma," she said quietly. "If changing schools will help you feel better and happier, then we support you."

Tears welled up in Emma's eyes as she felt a wave of relief wash over her. "Thank you," she whispered gratefully, feeling a sense of validation and support from her parents.

Her father nodded, his expression filled with determination. "We'll look into transferring you to a new school," he promised, his voice firm yet reassuring. "Your well-being is our priority."

In the days that followed, Emma's parents worked diligently to facilitate her transfer to a new school. Despite the administrative challenges and mid-session timing, they were determined to ensure Emma's smooth transition. Emma, in turn, found a renewed sense of hope and anticipation as she prepared to embark on this new chapter.

4

It was her first day of the new school and she woke up early in the morning, feeling a bit lighter. It was such a positive start to her day after adjusting to the new school. The fresh beginning brought a sense of excitement and anticipation for what the day would hold. Waking up early likely gave her a chance to prepare for the day ahead and set a positive tone.

She was all set for school and it was time for her breakfast. Her mother cooked Emma's favourite pancakes for breakfast. Her parents were overjoyed to see her full of excitement and without any worries.

Her father was ready to drop her off at school. Emma waved goodbye to her mother before heading out. Her mother gently touched Emma's cheeks with love and said, "I hope your day continues to be filled with positive experiences and new opportunities to explore and learn in your new school. All the very best, my kid."

It was a tender moment filled with warmth and affection. Emma was too happy and she replied, "Thank you mom, thank you so much."

Her mother was feeling great to see her embracing this new chapter with such enthusiasm and energy.

Her mother kissed Emma's forehead and said goodbye. Emma felt a sense of comfort and security in her mother's embrace, a silent reassurance of their unbreakable bond.

Emma's parents' love and support shone brightly as they embarked on their journey. Her father said, "If you encounter any difficulties or challenges along the way, please do not hesitate to inform me, my dear. I am here to help and support you in any way you need, my sweetheart."

Those words echoed with a sense of protection. His words reflected his love and commitment to being there for his daughter whenever she needed him.

Emma replied, "Sure dad! You are the best."

Her father smiled at her.

Emma stepped out of the car, on reaching her school. The sound of the schoolyard greeted her but her attention was quickly drawn to the principal making his way towards her as she entered the school premises. With a mix of curiosity and apprehension, she wondered what the principal might want to discuss with her but she kept herself calm.

Emma greeted the principal with a polite "Good morning, sir," to which the principal responded with a smile and asked her for her introduction.

Emma's introduction was a strong start as she confidently stated, "I'm Emma Parker. I study in 9th standard and I'm interested in science." Her words resonated, reflecting her enthusiasm for science and her determination to embark on an exciting educational journey. With this introduction, Emma set the stage for engaging experiences and academic growth in the school community.

The principal led Emma to the respective class and warmly addressed the students, "Good morning, students. She is Emma Parker. She is your new classmate and as she enrolled in mid-session, please help her."

With this introduction, the principal aimed to foster a welcoming and supportive environment for Emma to smoothly integrate into her new class, setting the tone for a positive school experience.

Emma's class began and she found joy in her studies there. Immersed in learning, she embraced the new academic environment with dedication. Her passion for science fueled her engagement in the classroom, making each lesson a rewarding experience. Now, It was time for a break, time had flown by, without her realizing. The moments seemed to slip away unnoticed as she immersed herself in the class. She was really enjoying her new school but she had her lunch alone and she became upset.

Suddenly, a boy came to Emma's seat and greeted her during recess by saying, "Hello Emma, I'm James Smith. I'm one of your classmates and I've been in the same school for 2 years. If you need any help then let me know it, I'm here to help you with anything you may require support with. Please feel free to reach out to me without any hesitation."

Emma expressed gratitude by saying thanks to James. Her appreciation likely made James gesture even more meaningful and then they both became friends. Emma was absolutely over the moon and the happiness came from forming a new connection and bond with James. Emma's enthusiasm was contagious, spreading positive energy and creating a joyful atmosphere. Her happiness was a reflection of the beautiful bond she had formed with her new friend and it was fantastic to see such genuine happiness and excitement in a new friendship.

Emma was savoring her class and she displayed exceptional intelligence in class, answering questions swiftly and accurately. Then, it was time for departure. Before going back home, she asked her new friend James for some notes. This simple request sparked a friendly exchange between them, leading to the sharing of their contact numbers which paved the way for future conversations and moments of friendship.

As Emma made her way home, her heart was filled with joy and excitement. A sense of jubilation enveloped her, brightening her journey with a radiant glow of happiness. Each step she took was light and buoyant. The memory of her newfound friendship with James lingered in her thoughts, adding an extra skip to her step.

As she arrived home, her mother's reaction was a mix of surprise and curiosity. Emma's beaming smile and the sparkle in her eyes caught her mother's attention immediately. She shared the story of her encounter with new friends, her mother listened intently. The excitement in Emma's voice was palpable, her mother was feeling grateful for the new friendship that had brought such joy to Emma's heart.

At night, they started chatting and since James was an introverted and shy guy, he was talking less during the conversation and he listened more than he spoke.

Emma said, "See you in school, bye James."

He replied, "Okay bye, good night Emma."

The next day, she went to school and felt delighted. James helped Emma in her studies and offered motivation concerning their exams. They were sitting together during recess and had their lunch together. It was time for departure and the bell rang, they went out of the school together and waved goodbye to each other. This was really a nice way to wrap up their day.

Another day, their holidays were announced due to the heavy monsoon. It was a bit unexpected but it gave them a break from school. Although the rain had disrupted their plans but they used that time to relax and spend more time online.

One day, James had a sudden realization that he had left one of his books with Emma, prompting him to inquire about Emma's address. Curious, Emma asked him why. He explained the situation, mentioning the forgotten book, which led to him making his way to Emma's house for the very first time. Upon his arrival, her mother warmly welcomed him and offered a cup of coffee. In that warm and inviting atmosphere, Emma and James shared a smile, a silent acknowledgment of their growing friendship and the beginning of a new chapter in their relationship.

They had a fantastic time during the holidays, staying connected through chats and calls. They used their time to study together over calls and support each other in their academic performance. Their dedication to studying together shows a strong commitment to their education and friendship.

Soon their holidays had ended and they returned back to their school. It was a bit challenging for them to transition from the leisure of vacation back to the routine of school. Both of them together created a schedule and both were very focused on studying as their exams were approaching. By dedicating more time and effort to their studies, they were setting themselves up for success in their exams.

Their exams were very close and they worked hard together to prepare. They were supporting each other and studying diligently as a team. They used to wake each other up at time and keep each other motivated. Working as a team made studying more enjoyable and less overwhelming.

Days passed in a similar manner and finally, they were in their exam hall. It was the feeling of a mixture of nervousness and determination as they sat down to tackle their exams. Emma indicated, "All the best & Stay focused and calm" to James through her hand gestures, James responded with a smile and thumbs up. A simple gesture of Emma wishing him good luck, boosted his confidence and morale. It shows the strength of their friendship and the care they have for each other.

So, after all the hard work and effort they put in, the moment finally arrived when their exams came to an end and both of them did really well and performed impressively, which left them both feeling happy and satisfied with their results. It was wonderful to hear that their hard work paid off and they were able to excel in their exams, bringing them a sense of accomplishment and joy.

Emma's parents were absolutely thrilled and filled with joy at the sight of their daughter not only reveling in the moment but also delivering a stellar performance. Their hearts swelled with pride as they watched her immerse herself in the experience and demonstrate her skills on stage. The sheer delight on their faces reflected the immense happiness and satisfaction they felt, knowing that their daughter was not only enjoying herself but also excelling in her performance. It was a truly heartwarming moment for the entire family to witness her shine so brightly.

It was time for their vacation, they both decided to stay connected through online means, ensuring that distance did not hinder their bond. Gradually, Emma and James became best friends. Despite physical separation during their vacation, technology bridged the gap, allowing them to share moments, thoughts and experiences virtually. Whether through messages or shared photos, they found ways to stay close and maintain their connection. Their conversation flowed effortlessly, filled with laughter and shared interests. happily looking forward to more moments of connection and camaraderie in the days ahead.

One day James decided to join the school bus so he asked Emma, "Hey! I think we should join our school bus. What do you think ?"

Emma replied, "It's a fantastic idea! We can join it from our new session."

James said, "Exactly! Plus, it will save our time. I'm looking forward to starting the new session on the bus with you."

Emma replied, "Me too! I'm excited for all the adventures we'll have on the school bus together."

After the conversation, they eventually made the decision to board their school bus. The decision marked the end of their discussion and the beginning of their journey together.

5

As their new session was on the brink of beginning, they secured their seats on the school bus as they had arranged beforehand. The anticipation of the upcoming school year filled them with excitement and a sense of readiness. The act of reserving their seats symbolized their commitment to starting the new session on the right foot, ensuring they were all set for the adventures that awaited them. With a shared sense of determination, they boarded the bus, finding their designated seat.

Time slipped away unnoticed and it happened to be their first day at school, traveling by bus. Their journey was filled with laughter and excitement as they discussed earlier. The bus ride provided a comfortable and familiar setting for them to bond with their peers and create lasting memories before reaching their destination.

After arriving at school, they walked together to their classroom. As they entered the classroom, their eyes fell upon a new student who had joined their class. The arrival of the new boy sparked curiosity and interest among the students. The students eagerly awaited the start of the school day. The presence of the new student added a sense of freshness among the classmates.

That boy was constantly staring at Emma, the prettiest girl of the class who wore eyeglasses and looked incredibly cute with her smile. Kaif's gaze was fixed on Emma without wavering.

Then the bell rang for their first class, all the students were ecstatic, their excitement palpable in the air. They couldn't contain their joy, some even jumping with enthusiasm for the start of the new school year. The teacher entered the classroom, but to everyone's surprise, she didn't notice the new student who had recently joined their class. Undeterred by the oversight, the teacher began her lesson.

During recess, Emma noticed the new boy who was constantly glancing in her direction. The repeated looks didn't go unnoticed by Emma, she was so curious about why the new student seemed particularly interested in her. She found herself alternating between feeling a bit flustered and intrigued by the attention. James also picked up on the situation and they both went to that new student and asked him, "what happened to you brother?"

The new student replied, "nothing, my name is Kaif." And then he smiled at Emma.

James went away from there and Emma also ran but kaif halted her and asked, "can I have your contact number? Actually I'm a new student and I don't have any friends yet." Emma wrote down her contact number for Kaif and hurried to run behind James.

Emma was showing her friendly nature and willingness to help out a newcomer.

Emma caught sight of James standing in the corridor. She walked over to him and elaborated on the situation, yet she inadvertently omitted to include the contact number in her explanation.

James shared his thoughts with Emma, stating, "Emma, you know, I don't have any issue with him personally, but I can't help but feel uneasy about the way he was just staring at you. It's not about any conflict I have with him; it's more about the discomfort I felt seeing his intense gaze directed towards you. I value our friendship, and when I see someone making you feel uncomfortable, it bothers me. I want you to feel safe and respected.

Emma held James's hand, and they walked back to their class together. During their mathematics class, Kaif asked Emma for her notes, which triggered James as he sensed that Kaif was trying to get close to Emma. Feeling surge of anger, James clenched his fist but Emma noticed his reaction and tenderly placed her hand on top of his, soothing his emotions.

The bell rang, indicating the departure and it was time to head towards the bus. James and Emma walked together to their bus, they both noticed that Kaif was also on the same bus. The unexpected presence of Kaif in their bus added a layer of tension to the atmosphere. Despite the situation, James and Emma remained composed.

Kaif smiled at Emma and said, "Hello Emma."

Emma responded with a little smile.

James, feeling quite tense, was unsettled by the intentions of the guy on the bus. His unease grew as he couldn't shake off the feeling that something wasn't right. Contemplating what actions to take next in response to the situation.

Emma had just arrived at home and settled onto her bed, enjoying a moment of peace suddenly her phone buzzed with a notification. Curiously, she picked up her phone and saw a message from an unknown number that was simply saying, "hey! I'm Kaif."

Emma, sensing that Kaif might be reaching her for help so she replied with a friendly tone, "Hello Kaif! How can I help you ?"

Kaif responded, "no no, I don't need your help, I just want to tell you something."

Emma, feeling cautious, replied, "please don't say anything stupid."

Kaif expressed his feelings, saying, "Emma, I really like you and I think I'm in love with you."

Emma retorted sharply, "shut up Kaif."

Emma found herself unable to concentrate on her studies, her thoughts consumed by the unexpected conversation with Kaif. In need of a break and some fresh air, she called James and asked him to meet her outside for a change of scenery and a chance to clear her mind.

Emma was driving the car but her usual cheerful demeanor was noticeably absent. Sensing his friend's unease, James gently inquired, "Hey! Is everything alright ?"

Emma, with a hint of sadness in her voice, responded, "I was not feeling well so just needed some fresh air."

Emma parked her car in front of a popular cafeteria and they decided to spend some quality time there. They were greeted with excellent service and a vibrant atmosphere which raised their mood. While they were engrossed in a conversation, Emma showed something on her phone to James. Ath the same time, the waiter approached their table, asking if they needed anything else.

Unbeknownst to Emma, James caught a glimpse of the messages from Kaif on her phone but he didn't let Emma know it.

James was deeply hurt and felt upset and because Emma didn't inform him about Kaif's message and neglected to mention that they had swapped contact numbers. The secrecy surrounding these interactions led James to question the trust and honesty in their friendship, leaving him with a sense of disappointment towards Emma.

James sat in silence, his thoughts swirling like a storm in his mind. Sensing his unease, Emma gently approached him and asked, "James, what's going on? Are you feeling alright? You seem lost in your thoughts."

James simply nodded in response, not uttering a single word. But his silence was speaking the weight of his thoughts.

Emma found it strange and speculated that James might be aware of Kaif. She silently thought to herself, "I haven't done anything, even though I didn't reply to him properly. Why is James behaving like this?"

Emma remained silent throughout their journey, with an air of quiet tension surrounding them. Upon dropping James off at his home, she bid him a casual "rukha sukha bye." In response, James waved his hand without uttering a word, maintaining the silent exchange that characterized their entire interaction.

Emma was also upset and when she arrived home, she headed directly to her room and drifted off to sleep. The unspoken words and the heaviness of the situation followed her into the slumber.

This went on for three days; Emma and James were together in school but were not speaking to each other. Emma was wrapped up in anger and James had also decided to stay silent, creating an atmosphere of silence between them.

One day, Kaif sent a message to her asking if she was interested in him or not. However, before she could respond, her mother came to Emma's room and asked her, "Are you not ready yet? Get ready soon, we have to leave on time." They were going to the celebration of her mother's friend's birthday party. Emma put her phone down and said to her mother, "Mom, please give me 2 minutes, I'm just coming."

Her mother replied, "Come fast, I'm waiting downstairs."

They came back late at night after the birthday party. Exhausted from the celebration and the late hour, she found herself drifting off to sleep and she forgot to respond to his message.

The next day, when Emma saw Kaif at school, suddenly she remembered that she had forgotten to reply to Kaif's text.

She didn't want to hurt James anymore, so she decided to share everything with him after their departure. And as the bell rang for departure,

Emma felt the weight of her unspoken words. She didn't want to hurt James anymore, so she made a decision to confide with him. As the bell rang for departure, Emma asked James for an outing in the evening. The timing seemed right, with the day winding down and the promise of a quiet evening ahead. Emma hoped that their time together would provide a comfortable setting for their conversation, allowing her to share her thoughts and feelings openly with James.

In the quiet of the evening, as the sun dipped below the horizon, Emma hugged James tightly, her words weighted with sincerity. "I'm sorry, James. I had planned to tell you everything, but it slipped from my mind. I know, you already have seen the messages." With a sense of honesty and vulnerability, Emma recounted the events of the previous day, revealing that he had directly asked her about her feelings towards him.

James hugged her back, providing a sense of security, and gently reassured her, "I was upset because you hadn't told me, but it's alright, Emma. Don't worry! I'm here for you."

Emma responded with gratitude, saying, "Thanks."

The air between them was filled with understanding. She felt a sense of relief wash over her as James's comforting words reassured her that he was by her side, ready to navigate whatever challenges lay ahead together.

James expressed his concerns honestly and said, "I didn't feel right about his intentions from the very beginning, and in my perspective, you should clearly tell him NO, buddy." His words carried a sense of protectiveness and care for Emma. James's advice, delivered in a friendly and supportive manner, reflected his desire to see Emma stand up for herself and set clear boundaries in any situation that made her uncomfortable. His words resonated with a sense of loyalty and friendship, emphasizing the importance of self-respect and assertiveness in dealing with challenging interpersonal dynamics.

James and Emma hugged each other and that was the moment when they had fallen in love. It was a time when their hearts intertwined and they began to see each other in a new light. The air was filled with a sense of connection and understanding that went beyond words. In that instant, the world seemed to fade away, leaving only the two of them in a bubble of affection. It was the moment that changed the course of their lives, marking the beginning of a beautiful journey together.

James wanted Emma to concentrate on her studies, so he asked her to attend an additional class held daily after school hours. They both agreed to participate in the extra class to enhance their learning and academic performance. Recognizing the value of this additional educational opportunity, they made a joint decision to commit to attending the extra class together. By choosing to invest their time and effort in this after-school session, James and Emma demonstrated their shared commitment to academic excellence and continuous learning. This decision not only reflected their determination to enhance their knowledge and skills but also underscored their mutual support for each other's educational pursuits.

Kaif found out that James and Emma were staying for the extra class. So, he too chose to stay and participate in the additional academic session with them. Kaif decided to align his academic goals with theirs by staying for the extra class.

The following day, as they went downstairs, James and Emma noticed that Kaif was already seated there. The sight of Kaif's early presence struck them as somewhat odd but they chose to proceed to their designated seats and commence their studies. That unexpected encounter at the start of the day added a unique twist to their routine, yet they remained steadfast in their commitment to learning and making the most of their time in the extra class.

After class, when Emma got home, she started thinking about everything James had said. She decided to pick up her phone and send a message to Kaif saying, "No, I'm not interested." Following that, she went ahead and blocked Kaif. Emma's anxiety persisted throughout the day, her mind consumed by the fear of something going awry. She was especially troubled by the possibility of a clash between James and Kaif. It was clear that she felt on edge in that situation.

Kaif's story didn't end here; he continued to bother Emma persistently. He also used to tease her every day at school. He kept requesting James to ask Emma to unblock him.

One day, James was absent because of his health, and Emma had no prior knowledge of his absence. When she entered the class she found James missing without informing her. This sudden revelation left her feeling upset and disappointed, prompting her to quietly proceed to her seat, trying to process the unexpected turn of events.

Kaif, taking advantage of James's absence, decided to sit beside Emma. With a gentle tone, he expressed, "Emma, you are truly a good girl, so intelligent. But please, could you please unblock me?"

Despite his seemingly polite words, Emma started feeling uneasy due to Kaif's persistence continued to unsettle her. His constant requests for unblocking and unwavering presence began to weigh heavily on Emma's peace of mind. This situation created an awkward atmosphere. leaving Emma unsure of how to handle Kaif's relentless behavior without escalating the situation or causing further distress.

When Emma came back home, she was feeling very tense. Her mother asked, "What's the matter? Why are you so upset?" Emma, with a melancholic expression, responded, "Nothing, Mom."

After dinner, feeling the weight of the day's events, Emma quietly made her way to her room. With a heavy heart and a mind full of thoughts, she reached for her phone and dialed James's number. As the phone rang, she wondered how he was doing and if he was okay. The sound of the ringing phone seemed to echo the uncertainty she felt inside. Each ring felt like a heartbeat, a connection to the friend she missed in that moment. Finally, James answered and Emma's voice tinged with emotion, greeted him on the other end of the line.

Emma chose not to disclose anything to James and instead engaged in a conversation about their upcoming plans. They deliberated on the topics they needed to focus on for school the next day. The discussion revolved around the coursework, preparing for tests, and ensuring they were both on track with their studies. As they exchanged ideas and strategies for the school day ahead, there was a sense of camaraderie and shared dedication to excel academically.

The following day, as they arrived at school, they engaged in lively conversations recalling about the previous day's events. Emma generously shared detailed notes from the classes that James had missed, ensuring he stayed up to date with the material. Throughout the day, they attentively participated in their classes and enjoyed each other's company during lunchtime, they shared their lunch with each other. Then the bell rang for an extra class.

They made their way downstairs for the class, Emma was hungry so she asked James to bring her something from the canteen. James returned with two steaming cups of soup, providing a comforting and warm treat for both of them. While enjoying the soup, a girl, who was one of their classmates, approached them with some dry fruits and said, "Hey James! I'm Samie," she introduced herself. James looked taken aback by the sudden encounter, but Samie quickly clarified the reason for her approach, "We are in the same project group and need to collaborate on an upcoming project."

James responded, "Give me some details, and we will definitely collaborate on this project together."

Samie asked with a curious tone, "James, if you won't mind, may I ask you, why were you absent yesterday?"

This question put James into an unexpected situation that led to his absence, prompting him to explain the circumstances behind his missed day.

Emma was just about to say something but James interrupted and said, "Actually, I was sick."

Emma found it a bit strange, but she didn't mind it. Suddenly, she noticed that Samie started sharing dry fruits with him. Emma didn't like this and she got up and left. James ran behind her and saw that Emma was standing by the window watching the rain. The sound of raindrops hitting the window created a peaceful ambiance. Emma's mind seemed lost in the rhythm of the rain, finding solace in its calming melody. James approached her quietly, respecting her moment of contemplation, he stood beside her, they both shared a silent connection, appreciating the beauty of the rain together.

Emma asked in anger, "why are you here James? Carry on with Samie."

James said, "It's beautiful weather, isn't it? I love the rain."

Emma and James continued to enjoy the weather together from the window, savoring the beauty of the moment they shared. Unexpectedly, Samie arrived and commented, "It's romantic," and swiftly went to the classroom. Emma felt a twinge of anger at Samie's comment but remained polite with James as they both headed to class.

Upon entering the classroom, Emma asked Samie, "What's your problem, Samie?" Suddenly, the teacher burst in, shouting, "What is going on here?" James took Emma from there to her seat. And they started to do their work and studied effectively.

The next day, James and Samie were working on a project assigned by their teacher. Emma also joined them and sat quietly there. Emma was observing them silently, then James and Samie shifted their focus to football. James asked, "Who is your favorite player?" Samie responded, "Harry kane, and who's yours?" Their conversation continued as they discussed their favorite football players and shared their thoughts on the sport.

Emma felt bad because football was her favorite sport and she had even been a captain of a football team. Despite knowing all this, James didn't involve her in the conversation. So she went back to her room and started crying.

Kaif, who was seated behind her, noticed everything and unexpectedly he commented, "Why do you keep looking back repeatedly? Is someone special sitting there?"

Emma realized that it was a taunt directed at her, which made her angry. But she knew she couldn't do anything to him within school premises, so she put her head down on the bench.

James was noticing everything, he was thinking of what to do next, suddenly the bell rang for departure.

They all were heading towards their bus and when Kaif stepped into the bus, James grabbed his collar and started hitting him. James's friends also joined in and supporting him. The commotion caught the attention of other students on board, creating a tense atmosphere. Despite the chaos, the bus driver intervened, separating the students and diffusing the conflict before it could escalate further.

Suddenly, their teacher followed the commotion and noticed it. He then sternly announced, "All you students will come to my office tomorrow."

But the fight between Kaif and James was not over yet; both of them called their respective friends and asked to meet at the bus stop.

One of their seniors stepped in and managed to defuse the situation, putting an end to the physical altercation at the bus stop and finally resolved the fight there, but the enmity of James and Kaif remained.

35

After watching that matter, James switched his project group. He took the initiative to approach their subject teacher and seek permission to form a new project group. With the teacher's approval, James decided to create his own group, which included Emma and some of his close friends. This change allowed James to collaborate with people he felt comfortable with and believed would contribute positively to the project.

While they were working on their project, a teacher arrived and announced, "The principal wants James, Kaif, and a few other students who were involved in the fight to report to the office." This interruption likely stirred up a mix of emotions and stress among the students called out by the principal.

On questioning the students involved in the conflict, the principal sought to understand the underlying reasons behind the fight. After gathering information about the situation, the principal made the decision to separate those students on the bus, to maintain a peaceful environment during transportation.

After their visit to the principal's office, James found himself deep in thought about Emma. The idea of leaving the bus left him in the thought of "who would then accompany Emma on the journey." Despite feeling the need to confide in Emma about everything, James struggled with how to tell Emma about everything. Emma noticed James in tension, so she asked about his troubled expression and the outcome of the meeting with the principal. James understood the weight of the truth he needed to share with Emma, he knew that it would upset her, once revealed. Despite the difficulty, he told her, "Emma, we can't come together now."

Emma asked curiously, "Tell me in detail, James. What did the principal sir say?"

James explained, "Principal sir separated our bus as a consequence of the fight."

Emma exclaimed, "James, why did you guys fight? Now, I'm going to be alone on the bus and I have to deal with the consequences because of your fight."

James's response carried a sense of protectiveness and he replied, "I fought with him because he was commenting on you and I won't tolerate this thing from anyone, whatever the consequences are."

There was a clear indication of James's willingness to take a stand and face the outcomes of his actions. He was prepared to confront the situation that arose from the altercation.

Emma was absolutely thrilled to have such a best friend who was willing to support her in any situation.

The happiness that enveloped her was incredible, knowing that she had someone by her side who was not only a best friend but a steadfast supporter in every trouble. The bond they shared was a source of strength for Emma, a beacon of light in both the brightest and darkest moments of her life. The friendship they had cultivated was a precious gem, Emma cherished every moment spent with her best friend, knowing that their bond was a gift to be treasured forever.

James had departed the bus and Emma had no another friend by her side. The empty seat beside her seemed to amplify her solitude as she steadily looked out of the window, lost in her thoughts. The absence of a familiar face or friendly presence left her yearning for connection, for someone to share in the moments of the journey. She was feeling the sense of isolation that weighed heavily on her during the ride.

After reaching the school, she felt better with James by her side. The comfort of having him by her side eased her worries and brought a sense of calmness to her day and brightened her mood. She enjoyed her day a lot.

As Emma's birthday drew closer, James embarked on the task of organizing and arranging everything for her special day. He planned a perfect gift to coordinate a memorable celebration. James put a lot of effort and thought into making Emma's birthday a truly unforgettable and amazing experience for her.

With each passing day; eventually, the momentous day came for Emma, which was solely hers. James extended a thoughtful invitation to Emma, proposing an outing in the evening, after school. This gesture showed James's attentiveness and care for Emma on her special day. Emma's heart swelled with gratitude for James's kind gesture, knowing that the evening held the potential for cherished memories.

Once the final school bell rang, indicating the end of the day, they reached their individual houses with a sense of relief and eagerly waited for the evening like an eternity yet filled with endless possibilities.

In the evening, Emma and James made their way to a renowned restaurant to celebrate Emma's birthday. The ambiance of the restaurant was warm and inviting, setting the perfect tone for their celebration. As they sat at a beautifully set table, surrounded by the aroma of delicious food, they shared stories and laughter, cherishing each moment together. When the time came to mark the occasion, a cake adorned with candles was brought to the table. With smiles on their faces, they joyfully sang "Happy Birthday" to Emma before she made a wish and blew out the sparkling candles. Then, James presented Emma with a beautifully wrapped gift.

Emma's eyes filled with gratitude as she unwrapped the gift. He gifted her a diary where he affixed their collection of pictures and wrote a heartfelt note below each image, serving as a reminder of the cherished moments they shared together. The diary became a treasure trove of memories, capturing the emotions and stories behind each snapshot, making it truly memorable.

The evening was filled with laughter, shared memories and the warmth of friendship, making it a birthday celebration to remember for years to come.

After cutting the cake, they decided to go to the mall for some shopping. As they moved forward, the twist of fate occurred – unexpectedly, they met Samie on the way.

Samie found out it was Emma's birthday, so she warmly wished her, "Happy birthday, Emma." Emma expressed her gratitude towards Samie and asked her to join them. Emma's gesture of including Samie in their celebration demonstrated her openness and generosity, making the birthday outing even more special.

They all together went to a mall and in a clothing store, James and Emma were admiring a beautiful dress. Meanwhile, Samie, exploring her own fashion interests, came across another dress that caught her eyes. In a spontaneous moment, Samie interrupted James and Emma's admiration, took him away from Emma, grabbed his hand, showed him the dress she had found and asked with a curious tone, she asked James for his opinion on the dress she had found.

James assumed that Samie was seeking the dress for Emma, so he began showing interest in the dress as well.

James, thinking that Samie was seeking the dress for Emma, so he decided to show interest in that dress too. In a subtle shift, he began to pay closer attention to the dress. But Emma didn't like how Samie snatched him away from her. This action left her feeling disregarded and upset, prompting her to exit the store in a state of frustration. As she walked out, Emma observed James and Samie deeply engrossed in their interaction, completely unaware of her departure.

Suddenly, James had a moment of realization and quickly made his way outside to find Emma. As he stepped out, his eyes fell upon Emma, tears streaming down her face. James approached her gently and explained that he had been specifically looking at that dress for her. James tried to convey his intentions and the misunderstanding that had occurred. Despite their initial intentions to resolve the issue peacefully, the confrontation took an unexpected turn, leading to a rift in their relationship at that moment.

Emma's emotions overwhelmed her as she stormed back home in a state of anger. On reaching her room, she expressed her feelings in a torrent of tears and loud cries, her voice echoing with the pain and disappointment she felt. Emma firmly held the belief that Samie had completely ruined her birthday. This conviction weighed heavily on her emotions, fueling her distress and amplifying the sense of disappointment she experienced. The weight of her words carried the weight of dashed expectations and hurt feelings, painting a picture of a birthday celebration that had gone terribly wrong.

Emma found herself in the depths of emotional turmoil as tears streamed down her face in the quiet of the night. Just then, a call from James broke the silence, Emma picked up the call and said in a trembling voice, "Hello, James."

Concerned by the sound of her tears, James quickly asked, "Emma, are you alright?"

Emma managed to express her distress, saying, "Dude, she spoiled my day."

The weight of her words conveyed the depth of hurt and disappointment she felt, showed a picture of a birthday celebration marred by Samie's actions. In that moment of vulnerability, Emma sought solace in sharing her pain with James, trusting in his understanding and support during a time of emotional upheaval.

That night, James helped Emma fall asleep, ensuring she was comfortable and at ease. Then he also began trying to sleep, knowing they both had school classes the following day.

All of a sudden, James received a message from Samie that said, "Hey James."

James thought that Samie might be concerned about Emma and would inquire about her well-being, so he responded with a simple "Yes, Samie."

Samie then brought up her concern, asking why Emma seemed jealous of their friendship. James reassured her, stating, "She isn't getting jealous of anyone."

Samie persisted, highlighting Emma's behavior that day and how she seemed uncomfortable with Samie's presence.

After Samie's last message, James chose not to respond further.

It seems like there might be some tension or misunderstandings brewing among James, Samie, and Emma.

The next day, Emma looked at Samie with a cold stare and avoided speaking to her. Samie persistently attempted to initiate a conversation with Emma, but Emma continued to give her the cold shoulder. Then, in an unexpected turn of events, Samie accidentally bumped into Emma and took the opportunity and said, "Dude, yesterday I had a chat with James about you."

On seeing Emma's emotional outburst, Samie stood frozen in disbelief. Emma's abrupt push and departure left Samie reeling, trying to process the unexpected turn of events. Emma, on the other hand, burst into tears and headed straight to James. In a fit of rage, she slapped him and her voice trembled with hurt and anger, demanding answers for his actions. She demanded an explanation and asked, "Why did you even speak to her? You know she hurt me before. How could you betray me like this?"

James found himself in a tough situation as he tried to explain the situation to Emma but she remained closed off, silently shedding tears in the midst of the classroom. James noticed everything but he couldn't help. Then, the bell rang for another period, interrupting the tense atmosphere. It was a challenging and heart-wrenching situation for James, witnessing Emma's distress yet being unable to provide the comfort or support she needed.

In the chemistry lab during their practical session, the teacher organized the students into group and by chance, Emma and Samie found themselves in the same group. As they worked on their chemistry experiment together, a sudden memory triggered Emma about what samie had done to her before, she acted as a barrier between Emma and James friendship. In a sudden and intense moment, as they handled the beakers, Samie forcefully grabbed the beaker from Emma's hand. Reacting swiftly, Emma slapped Samie, marking a dramatic turn of events in the chemistry lab. The atmosphere in the room shifted as the consequences of their conflict unfolded.

Then, the teacher questioned, "What is going on here? What was this behavior, Emma?"

Emma retorted, "She snatched it from me. If it got broken, then you'd scold me." With a mix of frustration and defensiveness in her tone, Emma justified her actions.

Emma had held onto a glimmer of hope that James would provide her with the much-needed support she craved. However, her expectations were shattered when James chose to remain silent, not uttered even a single word of understanding. The weight of his silence weighed heavily on Emma, causing a sharp hurt to her already troubled emotions.

Following her brief explanation, Emma swiftly exited the premises, leaving behind a tense atmosphere and unresolved conflict in the chemistry lab.

After some time, as the bell rang for departure, James made an effort to catch up with Emma but she was intentionally ignoring him, choosing to walk alone. While going downstairs, tears flowed down her cheeks. Lost in her sadness, she collided with her class teacher, the unexpected physical contact.

The teacher asked, "What's wrong, Emma? Why are you crying?"

Even though she was aware that her teacher was a person who would listen and offer support, Emma chose to remain silent and withheld her feelings. Emma decided to keep her thoughts and emotions to herself. Despite the opportunity to share her troubles with someone willing to listen, she chose silence and conveyed her feelings through a simple nod.

She went to her home alone and after arriving home, she started thinking about her day and crying, suddenly she noticed her phone was ringing and on checking her phone, she saw that it was James reaching out to her.

Emma received the call and didn't say anything but her sobs echoing through the phone. James asked, "Are you crying, Emma? Why?"

In a tearful voice, Emma responded, "Why did you do this to me?" And harmed herself with a blade in a moment of frustration.

James tried to calm her down, pleaded, "Please, Emma, try to relax. Allow me the chance to explain the situation to you."

At that instant, Emma abruptly ended the call, leaving James concerned about her well-being. James tried to reconnect with her, James dialed her number again but her phone was switched off. Determined to convey his feelings, he decided to send a heartfelt message, expressing, "I'm truly sorry, Emma. Today, I failed to be there for you. I was engrossed in a practical task and completely missed what you were going through. It was my fault and I promise you, I won't let it happen again."

James's message conveyed his regret for his absence during Emma's distress and a sincere pledge to be more attentive and supportive in the future. The message aimed to bridge the gap created by his unintentional neglect and reaffirm his commitment to being there for Emma when she needed him the most.

Emma was in a state of continuous tears after turning off her phone and eventually, she drifted off to sleep while sobbing. The weight of her emotions led to a restless and tearful slumber.

The next morning, as Emma stirred from her slumber, she directly reached to her phone and on glancing at the screen, she saw a message from James. This simple gesture of communication seemed to bring a ray of light into her day, causing her to experience a slight sense of relief and comfort. The message from James had a positive impact on her mood.

After seeing the message, she eagerly dialed James contact number, who was sleeping in his room. Surprised by the unexpected call from Emma, he picked up and promptly inquired, "Emma, are you okay?"

He was ready to listen and offer support to her. The connection between them in that moment was an evidence to their bond and care for each other. Emma, feeling reassured by James's immediate response, began to share her thoughts and feelings with him, grateful for his presence and concern.

Then, they made the decision to get themselves ready for school. The morning light streamed through the windows, casting a hopeful glow at the start of their day. Each step they took in their preparations brought them closer to the familiar routine of school life, a place where friendships were nurtured, knowledge was gained and memories were made.

So, when they arrived at school, the students found themselves heading to their first class of the day, which was scheduled to be a mathematics class but their regular teacher was not present. In place of the regular instructor, another teacher entered the classroom to take over as a substitute and instructed all the students to work independently on their tasks.

Emma was diligently practicing questions, fully engaged in her studies. On the other hand, James and his friends, feeling bored, began to make fun and indulge in a game of chits. Without including Emma in their activities, they immersed themselves in their own entertainment. When Emma turned back and noticed it, she felt hurt by the exclusion. Despite the disappointment, Emma made a conscious effort to brush off the feeling and refocus on her academic tasks. However, as the noise level escalated, Emma turned back and she saw James and his friends thoroughly enjoying their game, intensifying her sense of being left out. The situation made Emma feel quite upset.

Despite being surrounded by numerous students, she found herself in the sense of solitude. In the midst of the crowd, a pervasive feeling of loneliness remained within her. With only James as her sole confidant, the absence of meaningful connections weighed heavily upon her. James himself seemed distant, failing to uphold their friendship. This isolation compounded her emotions, intensifying the ache of being isolated despite the apparent presence of others.

Then the bell rang, indicating the next period that was 'sports'. the students began making their way to the sports ground. Among them, Emma lagged behind, noticing James waiting for her outside the classroom. She pushed him away, but James grabbed Emma's hand and stopped her. Concerned, he asked, "Emma, what's wrong?"

In response, Emma questioned him, "Don't you know anything?"

The tension hung in the air as they stood facing each other. Their eyes locked, conveying unspoken emotions and questions, creating a moment fraught with anticipation and uncertainty. Each heartbeat seemed to echo in the silence, amplifying the weight of the unspoken words hanging in the air. It was a moment frozen in time, where the unspoken tension between them spoke volumes.

James attempted to clarify the situation to her by stating, "I thought you were preoccupied with your studies, so I didn't interrupt you."

This explanation aimed to shed light on his previous actions. The words carried a sense of respect for her commitments, indicating James's attempt to be considerate of her time and priorities.

Emma replied with frustration, "Stop making excuses."

Her words carried a weight of impatience, indicating her lack of tolerance for justifications. The sharpness in her voice hinted at a deeper frustration or disappointment, indicated a desire for straightforward communication and a resolution to the underlying issues without the interference of perceived excuses.

James was about to say something, unexpectedly, two girls appeared, causing him to hurriedly depart the scene. He knew that those girls would likely mock them and spread rumors. His decision to leave abruptly was influenced by the fear of being the subject of unfounded rumors.

Emma went to the ground and sat there without saying a word. As she settled down, she noticed a football match in progress between two teams. Emma found a quiet spot in a corner and peacefully watched the game and she chose to observe from a distance. Despite football being her favorite game, she refrained from participating in her favorite sport with the players, a decision influenced by her current state of distress.

It was recess time and Emma was going through a tough time during the lunch break. While her classmates were enjoying their meals, she was in tears and hadn't even touched her lunch.

Overwhelmed with frustration, she took a blade out of her bag and harmed herself. Her concerning behavior did not go unnoticed by one of her classmates, named as 'George', he promptly reached James and relayed, "Brother, she is harming herself."

James was in the middle of his lunch and he quickly went to wash his hands, so that he could see Emma. While he was returning after washing his hands, he spotted Emma with a bleeding hand and she seemed to be heading towards the washing area to clean it. Reacting swiftly, James reached out to Emma, guiding her to the medical room to have her wound properly treated.

After getting her wound dressed, Emma swiftly withdrew her hand from James and made her way back to the classroom. James, not wanting to leave things unsolved, also returned to the class and tried to initiate a conversation with Emma. However, Emma was intentionally ignoring him, deep in her own thoughts. She was upset and sitting in silence throughout the class.

In the same way, Emma's entire day slipped away in sorrow and when she reached home, she cried a lot. She didn't even have her dinner and went to sleep on an empty stomach, feeling the weight of her emotions. Her hunger was overshadowed by the overwhelming sadness that consumed her thoughts.

It felt as though she was shedding tears daily. Emma and James found themselves in daily conflicts. Despite the frequent disagreements, Emma continued to forgive him, offering him yet another chance. Unfortunately, she found herself hurt each day as James repeated his mistakes despite being given the opportunity to change. Emma was left feeling uncertain about what her next steps should be, struggling with the dilemma of whether to continue giving James chances or to make a different decision for her own well-being.

She pondered the situation throughout the entire night and at midnight, she called James. Surprisingly, James was awake, his thoughts consumed by Emma. Instantly, he answered her call, his concern evident in his voice as he asked, "Emma, are you alright?"

Emma ignored his words and confronted him with a direct question, "Why are you doing all such things with me? Are you intentionally seeking to destroy me?"

Emma's question was laden with emotion, reflecting her confusion and distress at the situation. The use of such heartfelt language underscored the depth of Emma's feelings and the depth of the situation she found herself in.

James expressed his sincerity by saying, "Emma, trust me, I'm not doing it all intentionally. Believe me, every time I try to improve but I don't know why it keeps happening repeatedly."

Despite his efforts to make things better, he remained unsure about why the same issues persist. His inability to pinpoint the root cause of the issues added to his frustration, making the situation all the more challenging for him to navigate.

Emma extended her forgiveness towards him, demonstrating her willingness to save their friendship and relationship once more through her small but significant effort. They conversed for a brief period before eventually falling asleep.

The next day, they encountered each other at school, brimming with joy, as they prepared for their first class. However, their excitement was slightly dampened by the latencyof their subject teacher, who had yet to arrive.

Emma was standing at the door, waiting for the arrival of the teacher. The hallway was quiet and she could hear the soft rustling of papers from the nearby classroom. Suddenly, without warning, Samie hurried over and swiftly shut the door. Emma felt a sharp pain shoot through her hand as her fingers got trapped in the door's hinge.

Samie, realizing what had happened, quickly opened the door without uttering a word, leaving an awkward silence in the air. James, on the other hand, quietly observed the unfolding situation without offering any response. Emma, with a look of disapproval similar to a devil's stare, expecting an apology that never came. Her frustration was evident as she then turned her gaze towards James, hoping for his support.

Emma returned to her seat in silence and James was sitting behind Emma's seat, asked, "Is it hurting, Emma?"

Emma, visibly irritated, retorted sharply, "Does it matter?"

James was giving an explanation by saying, "Samie is my neighbour, I can't say anything to her."

Emma responded by asking, "Is it making any sense?"

This inquiry indicated Emma's engagement with the conversation, it reflected her thoughtful approach to seeking clarity.

Suddenly, the teacher entered the class. Emma was unable to concentrate during the teacher's lesson because of the daily events affecting her. While the rest of the students were actively involved in their studies. Emma's struggle to concentrate highlighted her personal matters that were preoccupying her mind.

James advised Emma to concentrate on her studies as their school life was coming to an end and final exams were approaching. However, Emma found it challenging to focus on studying due to the things happening in her life.

Emma was really upset and frustrated, leading her to express her emotions through abusive language. As she was taken aback by her best friend, James, leaving her at such a crucial moment. James was acting normally with everyone else except Emma. She was left by someone she trusted, especially during her challenging times.

Exams rolled around, Emma wasn't doing well as she usually did every year. Emma's academic performance has been impacted by her relationship and shattered trust she experienced. Even James's friends noticed a change in Emma's usual brilliance and were commenting on it. It was tough for her because her personal issues spill over into academic life, affecting her usual capabilities and performance.

Their school life had come to an end following the completion of their exams. Now, it was the moment to transition into university life. With school behind them, they were ready to embark on a new chapter in their academic journey.

James reached out to Emma with a message, asking, "Which university are you planning to join?"

Emma replied, "Dude, we will be heading to different universities and you will be happy."

James: "Why are you saying this? We are best friends and we love each other. How can I be happy being separated from you?"

Emma: "When we were in the same class, we were together and even after being my best friend you didn't support me, so it's better this way for you now."

James: "Emma, I didn't mean to do it. I told you before that I couldn't figure out why things went wrong. Please, Emma, trust me, I really did my best."

Emma: "James, I understand that you didn't do it on purpose. It's just been tough for me to deal with everything. I want to trust you but it's hard sometimes. I appreciate you trying your best, but I need some time to process everything."

James: "I promise you, dude, that I won't do anything like this again. I'll definitely improve myself but please don't leave me. You are the best person I have."

Emma: "James, I appreciate your promise and your willingness to change. It means a lot to me. I won't leave you, let's focus on making things right. Your friendship is important to me too."

James and Emma managed to save their friendship and relationship after that conversation, ultimately preserving their deep love and strong connection. They were willing to do anything to keep their bond intact. However, they were now faced with the challenge of attending different universities. Despite the upcoming separation, their unwavering bond and genuine care for each other provided a solid foundation to support each other through this new chapter in their lives. They cherished their love and maintained their special connection despite the distance that lay ahead.

Emma decided to enroll at the University of Roehampton as this university is known for providing high-quality education. The academic staff at Roehampton are experienced and dedicated to delivering excellent education to students. The University of Roehampton's campus is known for its beautiful and picturesque surroundings. The campus provides a peaceful and conducive environment for studying and socializing. At the University of Roehampton, teaching methods are diverse and tailored to provide an engaging learning experience for students.

While, James decided to get into london south bank university (LSBU). Campus life is bustling with various student activities. The university provides modern facilities such as libraries, sports centers and social spaces for students to utilize.

Even though they were physically distant from each other, their souls remained closely connected, bridging the gap that mere distance had imposed. Their souls intertwined, resonating with each other's thoughts and emotions despite the vast expanse between them.

Under the twinkling stars of the night, Emma found herself in a moment of reflection as she sat outside in the garden of her house, deep in thought about James. She whispered to herself, "James is truly a good guy. Yes, he makes mistakes and sometimes he hurts me too but he never does anything intentionally. I believe I shouldn't give up on him and on our relationship. There's a genuine connection between us that transcends the challenges we face and I believe in our ability to overcome them together."

She picked up her phone, her fingers tapping out a message to James, the familiar greeting of "hey James" appearing on the screen. Despite any past difficulties, this small gesture represented a step towards understanding.

James was also awake at that moment, swiftly responding to Emma's message with a warm greeting, "Hello Emma, how are you? I was just thinking of you, you know." In those words, he revealed a sense of fondness and care for her, a subtle hint at the special place she held in his thoughts. This spontaneous reply carried an underlying message of connection and affection.

Emma responded with a simple affirmation, "I'm good," signifying a sense of well-being in that moment. Then, she asked, "James, are we always together?"

James replied, "Yes, we are always together. Even when we're apart, our connection and friendship keep us close."

Emma said, "It makes me feel warm inside knowing that no matter where we are, we're always connected. It's reassuring to have a friendship like ours. Thank you for being such a supportive friend."

James gently advised Emma, "It's getting late, Emma. I think it's time for you to rest and get some sleep now."

Emma replied, "Yes, I'm going to sleep and you should sleep too. Good night."

James began to contemplate his next steps and said to himself, "Now I have to make her happy and fulfill her expectations, no matter what." He made a firm decision within himself.

This internal commitment reflects a strong sense of dedication and care towards Emma's well-being and satisfaction. James's resolve to prioritize Emma's happiness underscores a thoughtful and considerate approach to their relationship, aiming to meet her needs and desires.

Emma's experience at the University of Roehampton was transformative as she encountered numerous new faces and blossoming into new friendships along the way. The shift from her structured school life to the dynamic environment of college brought her a sense of joy and a significant departure from her past experiences. She absolutely loved the vibe and true energy of this new chapter in her life.

Emma and James were studying at separate universities, which made it challenging for them to meet up every day. They tried to make time for each other on weekends but as the academic pressure increased, their meetings became less frequent, happening only once or twice a month. However, they made a conscious effort to stay connected by chatting or talking on the phone every day, ensuring that their friendship remained strong despite the distance between them. They were maintaining their bond and supporting each other through their busy schedules.

As time went on, things between Emma and James started to change, leading to arguments over minor issues. Emma's anger escalated day by day, affecting her mental well-being. Eventually, the demands of their studies reached a point where they couldn't even find the time to talk daily. The increasing academic pressure and the tensions in their relationship created a barrier that hindered their ability to communicate regularly. Growing conflicts in their relationship made it difficult for them to maintain their previous level of closeness and communication.

One day, Emma was enjoying a cup of coffee with her friends after class. In the midst of laughter and chatter, her phone rang and upon seeing James's name on the screen, she was absolutely thrilled and swiftly picked up the call.

When Emma picked up the phone, James was all like, "Hey, Emma, listen, things aren't going well between us. We're arguing all the time and I see you crying a lot because of me. I think it might be time for us to end things here."

Emma was just about to say something, James straight up ended the call, leaving Emma in tears. Despite feeling upset, Emma was pretending to be happy when she was around her friends because she didn't want them to know what had happened between her and James. It was difficult for her to hide her true emotions but she didn't want her friends to get involved in her personal issues.

She tried to maintain a cheerful front, even though inside she was hurting from the sudden end of her relationship with James.

Since it was Christmas time, her vacation started and she was totally into the Christmas vibes. However, this year was a bit off for her because it was the first time she wasn't really feeling the magic of the season. In spite of her love for Christmas, Emma found herself not enjoying it as she usually did.

Emma felt the urge to share her feelings with someone, so she made the choice to seek help and support from David. Emma realized that she needed a listening ear and a supportive presence during this tough time, and she trusted David to be that person for her.

David and Verek were friends with James since school days. Back then, they weren't friends with Emma but now they've become mutual friends with her.

She got in touch with David and laid out the entire situation. In response, David comforted her, saying, "Emma, don't worry, I'll definitely talk to him and find out why he's acting this way." It's reassuring to have a friend like David who's willing to step in and help out when things get tough.

After the Christmas break, she wasn't really in the mood to go anywhere, not even to college but she had to because of her exams. Stepping foot on her university campus, she gradually discovered that word had spread like wildfire and everyone seemed to know about her recent breakup. It was challenging for her to handle not just the exams but also the added pressure of everyone being aware of her personal situation.

One of her classmates, Sherry, who had a soft spot for Emma, saw an opening after her breakup and decided to shoot his shot by proposing to her. Sherry didn't waste time in expressing his feelings for Emma, taking advantage of the situation to make his move.

It was quite a surprise for Emma to navigate not only the aftermath of her breakup but also the unexpected romantic gesture from Sherry. She was really mad but she kept her composure and politely declined Sherry's proposal with a firm "no."

After returning to her home, she found herself overwhelmed with emotions, leading to a cascade of tears that persisted throughout the night. The solitude of the night provided a space for her to release the pent-up feelings she had been holding in. Then, she picked up the pen and started writing a heartfelt note in her diary.

She wrote, "James, I love you, I really do. I wish I could just pause when I'm with you and stay that way forever. I need you, James, and I always will. I love you forever and always; no one else could ever take my heart the way you took it. You are my everything, please come back James."

After writing, she tore the page from her diary, crumpled it in her hand and tossed it into the dustbin. As tears streamed down her cheeks, she cried out in anguish, her voice filled with longing and desperation, "James, please come back." The echoes of her plea reverberated in the room, carrying the weight of her emotions and the ache of her heart.

Suddenly, her phone buzzed and she noticed it was David calling at an unusual hour. With tears in her eyes, she quickly wiped them away, composing herself before answering the call. She felt a mix of emotions - surprise, concern, and curiosity - as she accepted the call, unsure of what awaited her on the other end of the line.

David's voice broke the silence of the dark hours, saying, "I'm sorry to disturb you at this hour but I felt the need to inform you that today I had a discussion with James about you," he began.

As she listened intently, a mix of emotions flooded her thoughts, unsure of what the conversation might entail.

David continued, "James remained silent throughout our exchange, he didn't say anything."

Emma found herself overwhelmed by emotion once more. The news she had just received stirred a storm of emotions within her, leaving her heart heavy and her thoughts in turmoil.

She decided to get in touch with Verek to share all those things she was facing. She was waiting for the morning to contact him

The night passed slowly, each moment feeling like an eternity as she counted down the hours until she could finally connect with Verek and lay bare the emotions that had been swirling within her.

When the morning light filtered through the curtains, she made the decision to reach out to Verek. Opening up to him, Emma shared the entire story, expressing her need for emotional and mental support during this challenging time.

In the beginning, Verek's attitude gave her a feeling of empathy and motivation as he delved into the circumstances. His initial support, offered a ray of hope to Emma, reassuring her that she had someone by her side during this challenging time.

After a period of time had passed, Verek's true nature came to light. His initial facade of understanding and support crumbled away, replaced by the behaviour that made Emma's situation even more struggling instead of offering the comfort and encouragement she had initially received. He also tormented her due to his genuine affection and love for James.

Emma said to Verek, "Don't tell me how I should feel, until you are me or in my situation. We all have different levels of sensitivity." Her statement to Verek carried a powerful message about the human emotions. Emma's words conveyed a deep sense of personal boundaries and a plea for understanding.

But Verek's actions made her realise not to rely on anyone, not even the person who holds the highest level of trust. The impact of Verek's actions led her to understand the importance of self-sufficiency. Her experience showed her just how vulnerable it could make you feel when you rely completely on someone.

Emma felt a sense of abandonment and betrayal, her friends left her feeling alone and disappointed. She let out a piercing scream, her voice echoing through the room. "God, why is it always me?" she cried out, the frustration evident in her tone. She didn't know, why she was constantly facing such challenges. The room filled with the raw emotion of her plea, a mix of anger, confusion and a deep-seated sense of injustice.

She was feeling scared and tired at the same time, she had no urge to be productive. She didn't want to be socialise but needed someone to be with her. She was feeling paralyzing numb.

She couldn't imagine how much disrespect she had tolerated just because of the fact that she was in love. She was feeling unappreciated and undervalued in the process. James led her to the situation where she tolerated more than she should.

All the progress she had made was undone, like it never happened.

The professor, a figure of authority and knowledge, appeared genuinely shocked by the worse performance of Emma, as she used to be a brilliant girl in the beginning. It was a real curveball for the professor because it was so unexpected from Emma.

But no one knew that she was struggling with her mental health, which made it incredibly difficult for her to concentrate on her studies. The constant battle with her inner thoughts and feelings created a barrier that hindered her ability to engage with her studies effectively.

Emma became both mentally and physically weak. The weight of feeling mentally drained and physically worn out pushed her into a corner of isolation, where she was fighting a solo fight against numerous obstacles. The world had become a daunting place for her.

Emma wanted to focus on her studies so she decided to study with Cherry, who was the topper of their batch. So, she reached out to Cherry and asked, "Cherry, can you please teach me? Actually, I can't focus on my studies because of my health. So please...."

Cherry: "Of course, don't worry Emma! I'm here to support you.

Emma and Cherry made a schedule and decided to study near the lake for a peaceful study environment. By choosing that peaceful setting, they were aiming to create a conducive environment for learning, away from distractions and noise.

So, they headed to the location after their class and started studying. Unfortunately, Emma fainted while studying, and Cherry got worried. She tried to help Emma regain consciousness by sprinkling water on her, but Emma was still unconscious. It was crucial to prioritise Emma's health and safety, and seeking professional help. So Cherry took quick action and called an ambulance and then accompanied Emma to the hospital for immediate medical attention.

Cherry consulted the doctor and shared all the details about Emma's health. By sharing Emma's health history and the events leading up to her fainting episode, Cherry helped the doctor make informed decisions about Emma's treatment.

The doctor advised to admit Emma to the hospital for further care. Admitting her to the hospital will allow medical professionals to keep a close eye on her condition.

Cherry made the decision to stay by Emma's side in the hospital. It was comforting and supportive for Emma to have someone by her side during this time. Cherry was in a tough spot, confused between reaching out to her parents or her friends for help.

After thinking a lot, Cherry decided not to reach out to anyone and instead choosing to help Emma on her own. She knew that her parents would worry upon hearing about Emma's health and her friends would turn the situation into gossip. By taking matters into her own hands, Cherry showed independence and a strong sense of responsibility towards Emma.

Cherry was so engrossed in Emma's medical tests and taking care of her that she lost track of time, and before she knew it, night had fallen. Emma was conscious, but Cherry gently encouraged her to sleep again as her body needed rest to heal quickly.

Suddenly, Emma's phone buzzed, and Cherry noticed it was a call from Emma's mother. Cherry answered the call and greeted Emma's mother, saying, "Hello, aunty, I'm Cherry, Emma's friend." By identifying herself clearly and politely as Emma's friend, she established a familiar and courteous tone for the conversation.

Emma's mother greeted Cherry and introduced herself by saying, "hello Cherry, I'm Emma's mom."

Cherry responded promptly, saying, "yes tell me, how I can help you."

Emma's mother, concerned about her daughter, inquired, "Emma didn't reach home yet. I'm getting really concerned about her. Do you have any clue where she might be?"

Cherry: "No worries, aunty, she is with me, and we are studying together. I think she forgot to inform you about this plan, and she is going to do a night stay here."

Emma's mother: "Thank you for letting me know, Cherry. Please make sure she gets enough rest and studies well."

Cherry: "Of course, aunty. I'll make sure Emma gets a good night's rest and studies effectively. We'll work on our assignments together and ensure she's well-prepared for everything."

Emma's mother: "That's great to hear. I trust both of you to manage the study session responsibly. Bye Cherry."

Cherry replied, "Bye aunty, take care!"

Cherry, after hanging up the call, breathed a sigh of relief and quietly expressed her gratitude, saying, "Thank God." She felt a sense of relief that her mother didn't know about Emma's health, realizing that her mother would have been quite worried if she had found out.

Cherry, feeling responsible, quickly dialed her parents' number. When her mother answered, Cherry apologized, saying, "Hello mom, I'm sorry I forgot to tell you earlier, but I planned to study at Emma's house with her. I'll be staying over for the night as well."

Cherry, in a complex web of secrets, decided to withhold the full truth from her parents as well to avoid causing any unnecessary worry about Emma's health. Also, she chose not to disclose the details of James and Emma's relationship, a secret known only to her close friends. Cherry was protecting the privacy of Emma's relationships.

After a chaotic day filled with secrets, concerns, and hospital visits, Cherry finally found solace in a peaceful night's sleep.

The next day, Emma was discharged from the hospital with strict instructions from the doctor to avoid stress and excessive strain. The doctor also prescribed medications to support Emma's recovery and well-being. It was crucial for Emma to prioritize her health to ensure a smooth and speedy recovery.

Cherry arranged a ride for Emma and accompanied her on the journey back home. During the ride, Cherry took the opportunity to have a heartfelt conversation with Emma, explaining why she had chosen to keep Emma's health situation private. Cherry shared with Emma that she had not disclosed the details of her health to anyone, emphasizing her desire to shield Emma from unnecessary worry and concern.

Emma responded to Cherry's explanation with gratitude and understanding, acknowledging Cherry's support and care. She expressed her appreciation by saying, "Yes, I get your point, Cherry, and thank you so much, dude, for helping me a lot."

After dropping Emma off at her home, Cherry made sure to remind Emma to take her medicines properly and to take good care of herself. She urged Emma to be diligent in looking after her health and well-being, knowing that proper medication adherence and self-care practices were essential for Emma's recovery and overall health.

Emma replied, "okay, now you don't have to worry. I'll manage everything and I'm thankful to you from the depth of my heart. Thank you so much, Cherry." She expressed her heartfelt gratitude to Cherry, acknowledging the support and care she had received.

Cherry replied, "mention not dude, it's my pleasure. Now go and have some rest, see you in college, take care."

But after some days, Emma started feeling depressed. She found herself slipping back into the depths of despair, sinking into the same dark pit of hopelessness she had struggled to escape from. It felt like an uphill battle, an endless struggle against the difficulties. Her mental health worsened with each passing day. The constant battle against her inner demons and the external pressures she encountered left her feeling increasingly overwhelmed and unable to find respite. Each day seemed to bring a new wave of anxiety and despair, degrading her sense of peace and stability. The gradual decline in her mental health was evident that she was struggling to cope with the mounting stress and uncertainty. The darkness that enveloped her mind grew thicker and more suffocating, making it harder for her to see a way out of the darkness that seemed to be closing in around her.

Her frustration kept on elevating, and she turned into a girl dealing with a lot of anger issues. She began experiencing panic attacks and was diagnosed with bipolar disorder. This led to a challenging situation where her emotions were all over the place, swinging between extreme highs and lows. The combination of anger issues, panic attacks, and bipolar disorder created a complex web of emotions that she was struggling with.

She was feeling completely hopeless about her career and health at the same time. Her frustration continued to escalate, leading her to lash out at those around her.

9

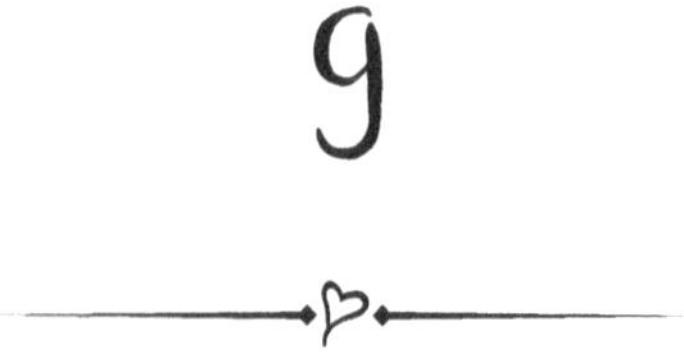

Emma found herself struggling to control her emotions in the university while dealing with anger issues. She easily got frustrated with classmates or professors, leading to tense interactions. She started to get irritate over little things. Even the smallest inconveniences could trigger her frustration. Whether it was a minor change in plans, a misplaced item, or a simple misunderstanding, her irritation would quickly escalate. This heightened sensitivity to small issues not only affected her mood but also strained her relationships with those around her.

Even at her home, she began engaging in frequent arguments with her parents over silly things, indicating a heightened level of stress within herself.

Emma's constant frustration was like a dark cloud that followed her at every step of the way. Her irritation had become her constant companion, accompanying her from sunrise to sunset. Whether it was a minor inconvenience or a major setback, Emma's frustration seemed to be constant.

Emma's parents noticed the visible signs of distress in her behavior like increased irritability, frequent arguments, and her frustration. They also noticed that she had become more withdrawn and distant, lost interest in activities she once enjoyed, and spent more time alone in her. Her appetite had also changed, either eating significantly more or less than usual.

Emma's parents, who knew her well, could see that something was amiss and that their daughter was struggling with her emotions. Their concern grew as they witnessed the impact of

Emma's distress on her daily life. This heightened awareness of Emma's emotional state prompted her parents to try to understand and support her through these challenging times.

One day, when they were all gathered for dinner together as they usually did, Emma had another argument with her family, this time with her mother over a little thing. She was feeling really upset to leave her food and headed towards her room. But her father intervened and stopped her by saying, "My kid, come back." As he wanted to prevent the situation from escalating further.

Emma came back to her seat as she respected her parents a lot. However, she was still seething with anger. She values and honors her parents' wishes and authority.

Her father kindly expressed, "Emma, we are your friends; you can share anything with us." His words carry a message of openness, trust, and support, creating a safe space for Emma to confide in her family. This statement reflects a deep bond of understanding and love within the family, emphasizing the importance of communication. It's heartening to see such a nurturing and compassionate approach from her father, encouraging Emma to feel comfortable sharing her thoughts and emotions with those closest to her.

She replied, "No dad, I'm fine."

She wanted to share her feelings with them, but she held back because she didn't want to cause tension or worry within the family. She chose to keep her feelings to herself to prevent any additional stress for her loved ones.

Her father replied, "Emma. Your feelings are important, and I want to support you in any way I can. So whenever you feel comfortable, you can share."

After the meal, Emma quietly headed straight to her room. She made her bed, smoothing out the wrinkles in the sheets with a sense of purpose. The simple act of tidying her personal space seemed to bring her a sense of calm and relaxation. As she fluffed her pillows and arranged her comforter, Emma took a moment to reflect on the day's events. The familiar routine of making her bed provided a moment of solace, allowing her thoughts to settle and her mind to unwind. In the quiet of her room, surrounded by the comforting, Emma found a moment of peace amidst the busyness of life.

After finishing up making her bed, Emma settled into a peaceful state in her room, the soft glow of her bedside lamp casting a warm light around her. As she lay there, thoughts of her dad's reassuring words echoed in her mind. With each passing moment, she found herself reflecting on the supportive presence of her father and the comfort his words brought her. Emma allowed herself to fully absorb the significance of their conversation.

Emma was contemplating how to open up and share everything with her parents. Despite having very supportive parents, she was afraid with the fear of being judged. Even with a strong support system, the thought of sharing personal thoughts and feelings was daunting.

Suddenly, it just came to her mind that day was a full moon, so she decided to head to the terrace for a walk under the moonlight. Walking under the moon's gentle light was a peaceful experience for her, offering a moment of tranquility and reflection amidst the quiet night sky.

For Emma, the terrace became a serene escape where she could immerse herself in the beauty of the moon's radiance, allowing her thoughts to wander freely under the celestial canopy above.

She strongly believed that a full moon night is the ideal time to let go of bad energy and release negativity, which allowed her to feel lighter, more at peace, and ready to welcome positivity and new beginnings into her life. In her view, the full moon's powerful energy has a cleansing and purifying effect, making it the perfect opportunity to rid herself of any bad vibes.

In the moonlight, she found herself lost in deep thoughts, reflecting on her father's words. Each word he had spoken echoed in her mind, offering comfort, advice, and a sense of connection even in his absence. As she immersed herself in the moon's gentle light, she felt a sense of solace and reassurance, finding strength and inspiration in the memories of her father's teachings.

She got tired during her walk, so she sat down on a chair, gazing up at the moon. As she sat there, the moon's luminous presence seemed to envelop her in a sense of peace and tranquility, creating a peaceful atmosphere that allowed her to relax.

In the moonlight, she whispered softly to herself, "I have no one with me, literally no one. And even after having my parents by my side, I feel like I have no one." And the moon was listening in silence, casting its gentle light upon her, offering a sense of understanding and comfort.

She unintentionally drifted into a peaceful slumber while seated on the chair. As she fell asleep, her breathing softened, and the calmness washed over her. The gentle rhythm of her breath matched the peaceful sounds of the surrounding environment, creating a harmonious symphony of relaxation. In her unconscious state, she was free from the worries and stresses of the waking world.

She woke up in fear, startled by a nightmare. However, she managed to stay composed and calm, choosing not to show any outward reaction to the unsettling dream. Silently, she got up from her seat and quietly made the way to her room, keeping the details of the distressing night vision locked within her thoughts.

She cried a lot in her room, feeling like she had no one to listen and understand her. The silence of her surroundings echoed her sobs and suddenly, she fell asleep while crying. The gentle rhythm of her breathing gradually replaced the sobs that had filled the room moments before. Her tear-stained cheeks, offering a temporary escape from the emotional chaos that had gripped her.

She slept peacefully at night, and consequently, she finds herself waking up too late in the morning. She quickly got ready for the university and asked Cherry to come half an hour earlier.

She quickly made her way to the university and arrived, eagerly waiting for Cherry. Unfortunately, Cherry encountered a slight delay as traffic slowed their journey.

Cherry elaborated on her situation with Emma, but Emma responded by saying, "Dude, leave it. I have to tell you something."

Urging Cherry to set aside the current topic as she had something important.tnt to share.

Cherry responded, "What's up?"

Emma shared, "Cherry, you know what? I think my parents found out about my mental health."

Cherry replied, "What did they say then?"

Emma replied, "They were saying that I can share anything with them freely."

Cherry said, "dude, then what are you waiting for?"

Emma hesitated for a moment before responding, then said, "I know, I just can't shake off this feeling of anxiety."

Cherry, with a reassuring tone, said, "I get it, but sometimes taking that first step can lift a huge weight off your shoulders."

Emma replied, "But, I don't know, how they'll react."

Cherry encouraged her, "Don't worry, they are supportive. Just be honest with them. It's better to open up than to keep it all inside."

Emma nodded, "You're right, I should talk to them about it."

As the bell rang indicating the start of their first class, Cherry turned to Emma and said, "Good luck with your discussion, you've got this!"

Emma smiled gratefully, "Thanks, I really appreciate your support."

Cherry patted her on the back, "You'll do great, just be yourself.

As they were going to their first classroom, Cherry and Emma engaged in light conversation, trying to ease Emma's nerves before her discussion.

Emma's day had been a whirlwind of activities and challenges. As she walked through the door of her home, a sense of relief washed over her. With each step towards her room, the fatigue seemed to seep deeper into her bones, making every movement a struggle.

The silence of her room enveloped her, creating a peaceful environment where she could finally let go of the day's stress and worries.In the dim light filtering through the curtains, Emma's mind slowly drifted into a dream-like state. The day's challenges faded into the background as Emma yielded to the comfortable sleep.

She woke up at dinner time, went to the washroom, and washed her face. As she stood in front of the mirror, the events of the day replayed in her mind. Cherry's advice echoed in her thoughts. The cold water cascading over her tired face provided a moment of relaxation. Each droplet seemed to wash away not just the physical grime but also the mental weight she carried. The gentle routine of washing her face became a ritual of renewal, a symbolic gesture of leaving behind the past and embracing the unknown future.

After having dinner with her family, she made the decision to engage in a conversation with her parents. The table was set, and the warm glow of the dining room lights created a cozy atmosphere. With a sense of determination, she cleared her throat, indicating her intent to address the topics weighing on her mind. Her parents, ever attentive, turned their focus towards her, ready to listen and offer their guidance.

She opened up to her parents about Samie and how their friendship had turned into enmity. Sitting across from her parents, she recounted the journey of their friendship, once filled with laughter and shared secrets. With a heavy heart, she detailed the moments of disagreement that had led to the fracture in their bond.

Then, she shared about Verek, how he was like a devil disguised as a human. With a shiver in her voice, she described the unsettling encounters that unmasked the darkness. As she spoke of Verek's actions and their impact, a sense of unease settled over the conversation.

In this manner, she revealed some of her pain without going into specifics. This approach of conveying her inner emotions without going into particulars spoke volumes about the complexity and sensitivity of her emotions.

Then they expressed to Emma the importance of staying strong and resilient in the face of difficulties. They reassured her that challenges are a natural part of life and that by persevering and facing them with courage, she would grow stronger and more capable of overcoming obstacles. They encouraged her to believe in herself and her ability to navigate through tough times, reminding her that she has the inner strength to overcome any adversity that comes her way.

They also explained, "as you mature, you will encounter a diverse array of individuals. They emphasized that along with personal growth, you would face various challenges in friendships as well."

Their words carried a message of understanding the complexities of human relationships and the hurdles that can arise within them.

Emma felt a sense of relief as she had the unwavering support of her parents. Their presence brought her a feeling of ease and happiness, knowing that they were there for her no matter what. With her parents beside her, Emma felt a deep connection and a sense of security that made her feel truly cherished.

But she didn't share anything about James which made her parents unaware of the full extent of her struggles. Still she continued to feel joyful and proud to have such supportive parents by her side. Their encouragement filled her heart with gratitude, despite not sharing all her struggles with them. Their presence alone was enough to lift her spirits and make her feel truly fortunate and blessed.

10

Emma started realising that she had to improve herself. She realized that personal growth and development were essential for her well-being and future success. She understood that by improving herself, she could overcome challenges, reach her goals, and lead a more fulfilling life.

This realization marked the beginning of a journey towards self-discovery and self-improvement for Emma, guiding her towards a path of growth, learning, and empowerment.

She experienced a brief period of deep reflection and self-examination. During this moment of introspection, she delved into her thoughts and emotions, contemplating her actions, beliefs, and motivations.

That introspective moment allowed her to gain her values, goals, and personal growth. She took the opportunity to reflect on past experiences, assess her strengths and weaknesses, and consider how she could continue to evolve and improve. Overall, this moment of introspection was a valuable and enlightening pause in her life's journey.

Emma's parents were filled with joy and pride as they witnessed their daughter's progress and the efforts she was putting into self-improvement. They were delighted to see Emma taking steps towards personal growth and development. Observing her dedication and commitment to bettering herself brought a sense of fulfillment to her parents. They appreciated her determination and the positive changes they noticed in her.

Emma was planning a solo trip to Holland. She was looking forward to exploring the beauty of Holland Park, a peaceful oasis nestled in the heart of London, the beautiful gardens, the presence of peacocks, and the Japanese Kyoto Garden. Additionally, the opportunity to relax by the pond and enjoy a moment of quiet reflection resonated with her desire for a peaceful experience.

When Emma arrived in Holland Park, she found herself immersed in a peaceful environment that welcomed her with open arms. As she wandered through the lush gardens and listened to the gentle rustling of leaves in the breeze, Emma felt a sense of peace wash over her. The beauty of the park enveloped her in a calming embrace, allowing her to escape the hustle and bustle of everyday life. The chirping of birds and the sound of flowing water created a peaceful soundtrack in nature. With each step, Emma felt more relaxed and grateful for the opportunity to enjoy her own company in such a beautiful setting.

Emma found numerous delights in Holland Park beyond its ambiance. One of the highlights for her was the captivating presence of peacocks roaming freely throughout the park. She was mesmerized by the elegance of those creatures around the park.

She was particularly drawn to the enchanting Japanese Kyoto Garden nestled within Holland Park. The pond was filled with colorful koi fish, the gracefully arched bridges, and the trees all contributed to the garden's harmonious atmosphere.

Emma found solace in the Zen-like tranquility of the Japanese garden, where every element seemed to be in perfect balance, inviting her to pause and appreciate the beauty of the moment.

Emma found joy in the simple pleasures of nature that abounded in Holland Park. From the fragrant blooms of vibrant flowers to the gentle rustling of leaves in the breeze, every aspect of the park's natural beauty capturing her senses. The symphony of bird songs, the sunlight filtering through the canopy of trees, and the soft caress of the wind on her skin created a sensory tapestry that filled Emma with a profound sense of peace.

At last, Emma's experience in Holland Park was a harmonious blend of peace, beauty, and history. From the majestic peacocks to the Japanese garden, from the Holland House to the simple joys of nature, every aspect of the park spoke to her soul and offered her relaxation.

After returning from her solo trip, Emma felt a sense of relaxation that inspired her to refocus on her studies to enhance her academic performance. The time spent exploring new places and enjoying moments of solitude had cleared her mind and renewed her motivation. She created a study schedule and set specific targets to deepen her understanding of challenging subjects.

Emma realized the importance of taking care of her mental health alongside her academic pursuits. Motivated by a desire for overall well-being, she included meditation into her daily routine. Meditation provided her a space for reflection, relaxation, and inner peace. Through regular practice, she learned to quiet her mind, reduce stress, and enhance her focus. The practice of meditation not only improved her mental health but also complemented her academic efforts by fostering a clear and calm state of mind.

Emma took several proactive steps to enhance her mental health and well-being. Along with meditation, she also prioritised physical exercise as a means of improving her mental health. Regular exercise and practicing yoga allowed Emma to release endorphins, which are known as "feel-good" hormones. Which helped in boosting her mood, reduce feelings of stress, and increase her overall sense of well-being.

Emma started focusing on self-care activities that brought her joy and relaxation. She started spending time in nature, reading books etc. Emma recognized the importance of taking time for herself to recharge herself.

Cherry's support for Emma during her mental health journey was incredibly comforting and empowering. Being there for a friend during such a hard time requires a great deal of compassion and understanding, and Cherry's presence provided Emma a sense of security. Cherry supported her by offering a listening ear without judgment and being a constant source of encouragement. Cherry's unwavering support made a significant impact on Emma's well-being. Having a friend like Cherry who stood by her side and supported her through her mental health challenges showed the true strength and depth of their friendship. Cherry helped Emma in her studies too which led to her progress.

11

She continued to work on herself to become even better. By focusing on self-development, she was investing in her future and setting herself up for success.

Emma and Cherry enjoying a relaxing time in their university garden, they both were talking and having fun together. Suddenly, Emma got a call from an unknown number, but she recognized it as James's number but she didn't tell Cherry about it and ignored the call because of Cherry's presence.

Emma was really curious about why James tried to get in touch with her. Her eagerness to find out the reason behind the call was showing how important James was to her. Emma couldn't wait to get in touch with James after her classes. When she returned home, she went to her room and dialed James's number. There was a mix of excitement, curiosity, and nervousness, running through her.

But James was occupied elsewhere and couldn't answer Emma's calls. She repeatedly tried to reach him, around 5-6 times, left her worry and concern about James's well-being. The unanswered calls added a layer of impatience to her.

Emma was going through a lot of emotions and uncertainties with James. She broke down into tears and started overthinking. She said to herself, "maybe he dialled my number by mistake. Oh God! Why did I even meet him, just for my temporary happiness? He made me happy and kept his friendship for a few months, after then he started behaviour weirdly, and didn't even support me. He always gave priority to others, He never valued me. Still I forgave him at his every mistake. I gave him another chance to improve himself every time. But what is the result of my efforts, he left me after 5 years of our friendship. Please god do something, I really love him a lot.

Emma was going through a deep emotional struggle regarding her relationship with James. She was reflecting on the ups and downs she had experienced with James, from initial happiness to feelings of neglect and disappointment. Despite forgiving James and giving him multiple chances, their friendship ultimately ended after five years. The depth of Emma's love for James appeared in her plea to God for intervention. She had invested a lot of emotion and hope into a connection that didn't turn out as expected. She really cared about James and wanted things to work out, but it was disappointing when her efforts didn't led to the desired outcome.

She was crying while sharing her thoughts and feelings. In the midst of her tears, her phone suddenly buzzed, breaking the heavy silence of the moment. She looked at the screen and saw James's number flashing on it. The tears that had been flowing freely moments ago now seemed to pause. It was a moment frozen in time, where her internal struggle and external reality collided, leaving her at a crossroads of emotions and decisions.

I understand you're looking for a longer paragraph. Here it is:

Without wasting even a single second, she swiftly reached for her phone and with a voice trembling with emotion, she uttered, "Hello, James." The sound of her own voice saying his name out loud in the midst of her tears felt like a blend of relief and apprehension. It was a moment where time seemed to slow down, each heartbeat echoing louder than the last.

James's voice carried a sense of regret as he softly said, "Emma, I apologize for all the things I've done." It was a moment where past wounds and present possibilities converged, leaving Emma in the confusion of forgiveness and introspection.

Emma said each word with the anguish of abandonment, "James, do you even realize the depth of my feelings when you walk away? I cried endlessly, day and night. Every passing moment was a symphony of tears. my mental well-being crumbled as I faced each moment alone. You were aware that you were my sole support, my only confidant, so why did you choose to abandon me in a stormy sea of troubles." Her words carried the weight of her pain and sorrow.

James's response carried a gentle plea, saying, "Emma, please, try to calm yourself. I can't bear to see you in tears; you know how deeply they affect me. I understand the weight of your sorrow, and I want nothing more than to ease your burden. Please, let's approach this storm together with calmness and clarity." James's words, infused with empathy and determination, ensuring that Emma felt heard and supported in her moment of sensitivity.

After calming Emma down, James gently asked, "Where are your college buddies? Weren't they with you when I left you?"

His words were filled with care and curiosity. James's concern for Emma deepened as he discovered that she was all alone, without even her friends by her side. That new information heightened his worry and shifted his focus to Emma's well-being.

Emma revealed a deep sense of hurt and betrayal by saying, "They all were selfish and cheaters. They left me abandoned when I needed them the most."

James listened attentively, absorbing the weight of Emma's words and the impact they had on her. He felt a surge of empathy towards Emma, understanding the weight of her words and the significance of the wounds left by those she trusted. He decided to support Emma through her struggles. He wanted to offer her solace and reassurance, to let her know that she wasn't alone in her struggles. James gently spoke, "I'm truly sorry to hear that, Emma. It has been incredibly tough for you to go through all of that on your own."

James continued by saying, "Emma, you know me well; I never intended to hurt you. I made the difficult decision to leave because I could see that you weren't happy with me. I realized that maybe I wasn't the right person for you. It wasn't easy for me, but I wanted you to find true happiness, even if it meant without me. I hope you understand that my actions were out of care for your well-being, even though it may not have seemed that way at the time. I truly wish you all the happiness and love in the world, even if it's not with me."

James's reply to Emma's feelings of abandonment was a moment of realisation. His response was laced with a profound sense of respect and consideration for Emma's emotions. He displayed a level of empathy and understanding that went beyond words.

Through his words, he demonstrated a rare combination of empathy, self-awareness, and emotional intelligence. His willingness to confront his own insecurities and prioritize Emma's happiness over his own desires proved his depth of maturity. James's response was a reflection of his respect for Emma's emotions and his commitment to fostering open and honest communication in their relationship. It was a moment of vulnerability and authenticity that laid the foundation for deeper understanding and connection between him and Emma.

There was an awkward silence between them, a moment where words seemed to fail them both. So James said, "Emma, please listen to me."

Emma responded, "Yes, I'm listening to you."

James expressed, "You are such a good girl; you always make efforts," he acknowledged Emma's unwavering commitment and kindness towards him.

James admitted his mistake by saying, "But what I was doing in return. I was constantly making mistakes and kept you hurting and crying. I wanted you to be happy; that's why I took the decision to leave you."

James understood that his presence in her life was causing more hurt than joy, which forced him to make the painful decision to step away, despite his own feelings. His words, filled with regret and self-awareness, revealed the complexities of human relationships and the sacrifices made in the name of love. The emotional depth of his confession underscored the profound impact of his actions on Emma and the sincerity of his intentions. It was a moment of reflection, realization, and ultimately, it was evidence of long-lasting strength of love in all its forms.

Emma's plea for a moment to contemplate the situation further, asked, "James, I need some time to think about it." That pause was indicting her intention to carefully assess all aspects of the decision and allowed her the opportunity to carefully weigh the options, analyze the situation from different perspectives, and ultimately reach a thoughtful and well-informed conclusion.

James's response to Emma was deeply emotional and heartfelt. He said, "Emma, you can take the time you need to make your decision. But I can't even imagine my life without you and you are not just a part but the entirety of my life."

After expressing his feelings so openly, James leaves the ultimate choice in Emma's hands, assuring her of his unwavering support regardless of her choice. He conveyed his commitment to Emma, reflecting the depth of love, and sincerity of their relationship.

In relationships, it's crucial to communicate openly and honestly, just as James has done with Emma. Sharing feelings and thoughts allows for mutual understanding and strengthens the emotional connection between partners.

Love is a complex and multifaceted emotion, encompassing care, respect, trust, and support. It's essential to be there for each other, to listen, to understand, and to stand by one another through thick and thin.

James was making amends, he took steps to correct his past mistakes. He apologized sincerely, and worked towards repairing the situation or relationship that was affected.

They ended the call, James was eagerly waiting for Emma's decision. On the other hand, Emma was deep in thought, reflecting on James and the words he had shared. As Emma was thinking of her next steps, she found herself confused, whether to forgive James and give their relationship another chance or to choose to focus on her self-worth and move forward without him.

On one hand, the idea of reconciliation with James brought a hope for a renewed connection, yet on the other hand, the prospect of prioritizing her own well-being and self-respect by moving on without him seemed equally compelling.

Emma's internal struggle reflected a deeper introspection about what she truly valued and deserved in a relationship, highlighting the internal conflict between forgiveness and self-preservation.

As she thought about it, she realized that that she had consistently offered James opportunities to rectify his mistakes and grow, always hoping for positive change. Now with the belief that he had come to understand her true worth, Emma made a heartfelt decision to grant him one more chance.

It was a big step for her, showing her kindness and hope for a better future with him. Her decision reflects her belief in growth and second chances.

The next morning, as the sun gently streamed through the curtains, Emma picked up the phone and dialed James's number. With a hope in her voice, she asked him to meet her, feeling a sense of urgency to continue their journey of understanding and growth.

They decided the time and location to meet, their voices carried a sense of excitement as they were meeting after a year. With each detail discussed, from the specific hour to the chosen spot, their connection seemed to deepen. As they finalized the arrangements, a sense of unity and mutual understanding enveloped them, setting the stage for a meeting that held the promise of new beginnings and the potential for their bond to flourish even further.

As they both arrived at their location, Emma's couldn't take off her eyes from James. He was looking more handsome with the glasses on his eyes, a touch of sophistication, framing his features in a way of intelligence and charm. Emma found herself captivated by this evolved version of James. That enhancement in his characteristics not only made James more physically attractive but also highlighted the inner qualities that made him stand out in a crowd.

James swiftly came to Emma and hugged her tightly. In that moment, the world around them seemed to fade away, leaving only the two of them locked in an embrace that spoke volumes. With a heartfelt tone, James uttered a sincere apology with weight of regret and a genuine desire to make amends.

Emma also hugged him back and then, they settled on their seats.

James asked, "Yes miss, what have you decided?" With a tone of curiosity and respect.

Emma expressed, "James, I'm ready to give you another chance, but promise me that you will never hurt me again." Her words carried a weight of past experiences and a glimmer of hope for a better future.

James replied, "Yes, I promise you with all my heart that I will never hurt you again. I'll make you happy, protect you, support you, and will always be there for you. I swear, I'll give my 100%. I value your trust and I am committed to making things right between us. Thank you for giving me this opportunity to show you that I can be better and we can be better together."

Emma replied, "James, your words mean a lot to me. It's comforting to hear your promise and commitment to our relationship. Trust is so important to me, and knowing that you're willing to go above and beyond to make things right fills me with hope. I believe in second chances, and I believe in us."

James and Emma embraced each other tightly. It was like a new chapter began for both of them, filled with promise and the potential for a stronger bond between them.

James and Emma found joy in each other's company, their happiness radiating from the newfound harmony in their relationship. James had transformed into a better man for Emma, showing respect for her efforts and a deep appreciation for her presence in his life.

Emma, in turn, was overjoyed by the positive changes she witnessed in James. Their journey together was marked by mutual respect, appreciation, and a shared happiness that brightened their path ahead.

Emma grew stronger with each passing day, as she embarked on her academic and professional pursuits, James stood by her side as a pillar of unwavering support, offering not only words of encouragement but also actions that showed his belief in her abilities.

Emma's focus on shaping a bright future was fueled by a deep sense of purpose and hope that guided her steps towards her goals. James's presence in her life served as a constant source of strength and reassurance, allowing Emma to face life's complexities with a sense of confidence.

With each milestone she achieved, Emma found validation in her efforts and a deep belief in her potential to shape her destiny. The journey towards her dreams was not without its challenges, but with James and her parents by her side, Emma faced each obstacle with determination.

The realization that she was on the right path towards her dreams brought Emma a sense of satisfaction. The foundation of love, support, and encouragement that James and her parents provided allowed her to flourish.

James went through a significant transformation for Emma; he truly evolved into a kind and caring individual for her. His impact on Emma's life was amazing. He transitioned from his previous self into a person who consistently showed kindness, support, and understanding towards her. Change in James not only influenced Emma's perception of him but also had an impact on their relationship.

Emma was shocked by James's transformation, leading her to question James about his appreciation for her. She asked, "How you suddenly recognized my worth as you never overlooked my efforts. I'm asking this because you have changed a lot." Emma's query delved into the depths of James's realization process.

James replied, "Do you know, David? He came to me, asked about you, and explained me your importance. He said that I'll never have a girl like you, who always stood by me even when I was not supporting you. Which made me feel a sense of gratitude and admiration for your support. David's message served as a wake-up call for me, and made a shift in my attitude to a respectful relationship."

David's intervention served as a powerful catalyst, illuminating Emma's support and loyalty even in moments when James himself had failed to reciprocate.

Emma asked with curiosity, "does it mean, you didn't realise it by yourself?"

James replied, "No! David explained things to me, I actually ended up realizing it on my own."

Then, James and Emma shared a delightful moment of laughter together after their realizations.

It was a special experience for both of them. Laughter brought them closer and created a sense of unity. Their bond grew stronger as they connected through understanding and joy. Those shared moments of laughter and connection were truly meaningful and memorable for them.

James opened up to Emma, sharing his heartfelt realization, saying, "Emma, to be honest, I realized your value on my own. When I left you, I found myself alone, and I also faced a lot of problems." James's admission not only revealed his weakness but also emphasized the essential role Emma played in his life.

James continued to pour out his feelings to Emma, by saying, "You are a lucky charm for me. I remember when we were together, you always shielded me from problems and challenges. You mean a lot to me, dude."

He conveyed a deep sense of gratitude and affection towards Emma. James not only revealed his appreciation for her support but also highlighted the impact she had on his well-being and happiness.

Emma replied , "I'm happy that you have realized my importance. Even though it took 5 years for you to understand me, but it's okay; at least you realized it. Thanks a lot, James."

James expressed his gratitude by saying, "Mention not Emma, you also did a lot for me, even you do."

By recognizing Emma's continuous efforts, James reciprocated the appreciation and emphasized the mutual exchange of care in their friendship.

Emma politely said, "One more thing, please make sure to deliver my message to David that I'm thankful to him."

James responded, "Sure! And a big thanks to you too. I was never deserving of what you did for me, you really did a lot. I'm really lucky to have you as my best friend and partner."

He expressed his gratitude towards Emma, his words reflected the deep bond he shared with Emma.

James and Emma have reached a point where they both appreciated the importance of each other in their lives. They feel incredibly fortunate to have found a best friend and partner in the same person, a rare and precious combination. They have remained loyal to each other, despite the challenges and obstacles that have come their way.

The depth of their friendship and partnership is truly remarkable. They have developed a profound understanding of each other, recognizing and valuing the unique qualities and strengths that they bring to the relationship. Their ability to appreciate and celebrate each other's differences has been a cornerstone of their enduring bond. Through their shared experiences and challenges, they have grown together, learning from each other and evolving as individuals within the context of their relationship.

The journey of James and Emma was showing the power of loyalty. Their commitment to each other went beyond mere words; it was reflecting in their actions and the way they stood up for each other, day in and day out. The level of dedication and mutual respect solidified their bond.

James and Emma continued to cherish and nurture their relationship. They understood the importance of communication, honesty, and trust in maintaining a healthy connection.

In conclusion, the relationship between James and Emma is a beautiful example of the transformative power of friendship and partnership. Their journey together, marked by loyalty, gratitude, and mutual respect, showed the deep connection and bond that can form between two people who truly value and appreciate each other. As they continue to face life's ups and downs together, James and Emma stand as a shining example of the enduring strength and beauty of a friendship that blossoms into a lifelong partnership.

One day, James and Emma walked along the quiet path that led away from the cliff, their footsteps creating a rhythmic pattern against the soft earth. The evening air was cool and refreshing, carrying with it a sense of tranquility that mirrored the peace they felt in each other's presence.

As they strolled side by side, Emma glanced at James with a gentle smile and they both reminisced about their early days together, the struggles and triumphs that had shaped their bond into what it was today. From the uncertainties of youth to the challenges that tested their commitment, they had navigated it all with a resilience born out of their love for each other.

"You know," James said thoughtfully, "I never imagined I'd be where I am now. You've been my rock, Emma. Through everything."

Emma squeezed his hand affectionately. "And you've been my anchor, James. I don't think I could have made it through some of those tough times without you."

They paused by a bench overlooking a tranquil pond, its surface shimmering under the soft glow of the moon. Sitting down together, they let the peaceful ambiance envelop them, a comfortable silence settling between them.

"I want to promise you something, Emma," James said earnestly, turning to look into her eyes.

Emma's heart skipped a beat, sensing the sincerity in his voice. "What is it, James?"

"I promise to always cherish you, to support you in your dreams, and to be there for you no matter what," James declared, his voice filled with determination.

Emma felt tears welling up in her eyes, touched by his heartfelt words. "And I promise to love you fiercely, to stand by your side through every storm, and to always believe in us."

They sealed their promises with a tender embrace, their hearts beating in sync with the promise of a future filled with hope and possibility. The journey they had embarked on together had taught them the true meaning of love and commitment, a bond that had grown stronger with each passing day.

As they sat together under the canopy of stars, James and Emma knew that their story was far from over. They had overcome the obstacles that once threatened to tear them apart, emerging not only as partners but as soulmates who understood and valued each other in ways words could not fully capture.

The night stretched on, a timeless moment suspended in their shared happiness. With a sense of gratitude for the journey that had led them to this point, James and Emma looked ahead to the future with renewed optimism and a deep sense of contentment.

Their love story was a testament to the power of resilience, forgiveness, and the unwavering belief in the transformative power of love. As they embraced the promise of tomorrow, James and Emma knew that together, they could face anything that life had in store for them.

www.ingramcontent.com/pod-product-compliance
Lightning Source LLC
Chambersburg PA
CBHW031318130726
47988CB00007B/2879